GHOSTS AND MYSTERIES OF BROWARD COUNTY

GHOSTS AND MYSTERIES OF BROWARD COUNTY

DOROTHY SALVO DAVIS + W.C. MADDEN

Published by Haunted America
A Division of The History Press
Charleston, SC 29403
www.historypress.net

First published 2010

ISBN 9781540234841

Library of Congress Cataloging-in-Publication Data

Davis, Dorothy Salvo.
Ghosts and mysteries of Broward County / Dorothy Salvo Davis and W.C. Madden.
p. cm.
ISBN 978-1-59629-873-6
1. Ghosts--Florida--Broward County. I. Madden, W. C. II. Title.
BF1472.U6D378 2010
133.109759'35--dc22
2010027743

Notice: The information in this book is true and complete to the best of our knowledge. It is offered without guarantee on the part of the author or The History Press. The author and The History Press disclaim all liability in connection with the use of this book.

CONTENTS

Contents

Acknowledgements

Throughout the process of gathering information and writing this book, I received a great deal of support. The friendliness and willingness to share information came from many individuals found in the stories on the pages ahead. If not for their courage to trust in the open minds of the readers, this book would not have been possible. My sincere thanks go to those that allowed me to interview them and glimpse into their personal lives.

A very special thanks go to my family and friends for their support. My husband, Chris: you are my constant encouragement. To my children, Victoria, Jasmine, Christian and Angelina: thank you for your patience with my seemingly endless hours working on this book. Chris and kids: you are my life's breath. To my sisters, Elaine, Paula and Josie: you really are the best gifts our parents gave me. Josie: you are eternally my best friend and closest confidant; thank you for believing in me. Conner, Kadalina, Bear and Michael have all moved me to leave an example to be proud of. Danni and Lyric Davis, strength and warmth shine bright in your eyes.

To my father Paolo Salvo: you are the most remarkable man I have ever known; through your example, I will always strive to learn and achieve.

My friends, Pat and Misha: I can't leave you out. The two of you are some of the most kindhearted and inspiring people I have ever known.

A very special thank you to the following groups for supplying information on local lore to supplement the many hours of historical

research among old newspapers and county histories: Fort Lauderdale Historical Society, Genealogical Society of Broward County, Broward County Community College Nova University–Paula Angelica, Fort Lauderdale Ghost Tour investigator–author John Marc Carr (very informative tour), Deerfield Beach Historical Society, Broward County Library, Coral Springs Library and Deerfield Beach Library.
Dorothy (Salvo) Davis

I would like to thank the Hoch Heritage Center for having a file about ghosts, which gave me some valuable information for this book. I'd also like to thank my wife, Janice, who is always by my side and went to Fort Lauderdale with me to help me research this book. And thanks to Dorothy for asking me to assist her with this book. And I thank the Almighty for giving me this writing talent.
W.C. Madden

INTRODUCTION

Broward County is known as a great tourist destination and a place to start a cruise. It's not so well known for its ghost stories. This book takes a look at those not-so-obvious attractions. The stories come from all parts of the county and from many of the cities within the county.

Some of the stories are connected to the history of the county, while others have absolutely nothing to do with it. One corner of the Devil's Triangle starts in Broward County, so there's a good reason for some of the ghostly tales about the county.

In any case, we think you'll enjoy reading about a different side of the county that's hidden from the tourists or residents of the county.

CHAPTER 1

FORT LAUDERDALE HAUNTS

THE HAUNTED ART INSTITUTE

The Art Institute of Fort Lauderdale has been providing students with the opportunity to reach the stars since 1968. Many artists have come and gone from the school in search of their dreams; the school was the start of many bright futures. Perhaps the desire to learn and achieve has been felt so great in some of the students that even after death they return.

On several occasions the spirit of a young woman in seventies-era attire has been seen walking the main entrance lobby. She is said to be tall and thin with waist-length straight blonde hair. She looks as real as anyone, but when she realizes she has been spotted she will freeze and make eye contact with the unfortunate witness. Then she is said to smile and fade away as if she were never there. Many students over the years have missed class as a result of being startled by the lovely apparition.

In the fall of 2009, two male students were approaching the front doors. As they passed the fountain in front, they stopped and looked in disbelief. In the decorative pool of water by the entrance was a small child. The child was a boy wearing old-fashioned bloomers and holding what looked like a wooden toy gun. The boys thought it very odd that a child would be left unattended and, even worse, in water! Their concern for the child turned to fear for themselves when, in only moments after viewing the boy, they realized that the building could be seen right through the boy's body! The two young, buff students turned and ran back to their car!

Spooky students are returning to the Art Institute of Fort Lauderdale. *Courtesy of W.C. Madden.*

Another ghostly apparition that has been spotted is a young man around twenty. He is said to have been seen walking at a fast pace with his head down. If someone enters in his path, he just walks right through them. This man has a backpack tossed over one shoulder and always appears to be looking at his feet as he rushes about.

Other occurrences, like doors opening and closing by themselves and wet footprints on clean floors, have plagued the school over the years. Despite the spooky events, the education at the school is very desirable. Perhaps that is why young apparitions seem to be drawn to the building.

FLORIDA'S VILLAIN REBORN

In the spring of 2001, Joe was in a job—that he quite frankly hated—at a local community car lot. His immediate supervisor was a red-faced, shrewish man who watched his every move and fabricated myths about Joe's conduct out of sheer spite. At the time, he could not know that within five years the place would crumble and fall amid charges of corruption, nepotism, graft and vice. No wonder he didn't fit in as he was an honest man amid vipers.

As Joe pulled into the parking lot that fateful day, he saw a cluster of crows poised in the distance around a puddle. He paid them no mind as he entered the building. Something told Joe to bypass the main office that day and just go straight to his cubicle before they got busy, but he did anyway—stupid man! He'd been pink slipped; they called it a reduction-in-force due to budget cuts but he knew better. The jack-a-nape in the office was all too happy to invoke the no-contest clause in his contract and send him on his way. After all, they could hire a lot more part-timers for the price of him, a full-time employee.

Somehow, Joe managed not to blubber like an idiot throughout the day. At least they had waited until a Friday; the reality of unemployment had not set in. Finally, it was time to go to his vehicle. The flock of birds was still outside. It had, however, relocated to his Suburban. The crows perched, cawed and menaced. Quite honestly, it was some time before he could shoo them from his vehicle. The odd thing was that his car was surrounded by a sea of other cars in a large college parking lot, and it was the only one covered by the bluish-black, gabby birds. When the birds finally left, there wasn't a drop of bird feces on his car. Joe didn't know why the birds left; it wasn't like he had a raven-covered car. Still, the episode gave him the heebie-jeebies—there was a message in the visit. He knew it, and he despised them. The urban legend that a flock of birds surrounding an area was a sign of misfortune or even death ran through his mind as he drove away; and there was the movie *The Birds*, an Alfred Hitchcock thriller in which birds attacked humans.

Joe went home and dealt with the gamut of emotions that goes with losing a job and a going away party thrown by crows. That night, he saw what he thought was a shadow of a man in the corner of his room, but he blew it off as a stressed-out mind playing tricks on him, since he was emotionally overwrought. Weeks passed, and he became depressed. He went through the motions of surviving his job until it ended and went home. Summer came and the job ended, and, while at home, he began planning for a new business; still, tensions ran high. He had financial worries and migraines, so he lay in bed most of the day.

Joe found an old storefront in an older part of Fort Lauderdale and began to make a career change altogether. The building had once been a dance studio, an auto parts store and a diner. It was old but had a good vibe—Joe liked the feel of it. The dilapidated building abutting the structure, though, was another story. It had been a speakeasy, a furniture store and a funeral home. Within a week of moving into the building, as luck would have it, the building next door was condemned. Local historians tried to prevent its demolition. They went into the basement one day and pulled out some unique caskets from the late 1800s—that was strange because the caskets predated the building. They were wooden caskets with little windows where people could look in and see the faces of the deceased. In Joe's building and the one next door, he never felt

Joe went to work in the older part of Fort Lauderdale near the historic district, as shown by this sign. *Courtesy of Dorothy (Salvo) Davis*

a particular entity, but sometimes he felt a heaviness and occasionally objects would fall from the walls. Knocking could be heard from inside the walls and strange tapping was heard from the windows.

All the while, Joe was working very hard and experiencing headaches and strange sleep patterns. At some point during this period, he began to start seeing the shadow person. At first it was like a head and a torso that would appear in corners or hop down the hall to his bedroom. At first, he thought it was the result of too much migraine medicine, but it would appear on hazy afternoons or in the middle of the night. Seeing this being would always cause him concern, but he always sensed that he was being watched.

One night, though, after a shadow man hopped down the hall, he decided to really concentrate on it and watch it carefully. That's when it began to do a lot of really odd things. It backed into a wall and broke into spider-like pieces and began crawling around the perimeter of the room. It didn't crawl arm over arm like a human would prowl but like one of those rubber toys when you slap it against a wall and it rolls down in a vertical fashion—only these did so horizontally.

When these shadowy beings appeared, it was mostly silent; occasionally, there was a sound like air leaking from a tire. Oftentimes, Joe's chest felt tight, like he was unable to move and he could not speak. Still, he never really believed what he was seeing. He really convinced himself that the strange events were hallucinations.

He didn't know if it followed him home from the new business, if it was psychological manifestations due to his stress or if the figures were indeed unearthly beings. One evening he closed up his business on Los Olas Boulevard and decided to take a walk. It was a perfect evening and the fresh air felt wonderful. Joe had just started walking when he heard a whisper in his ear. "Good day Joe," a female voice sounded.

He turned fast in a full circle and saw no one. Then, out of the corner of his eye, he caught a glimpse of his reflection in a window. Beside him was a woman in an old-fashioned 1920s dress. She hovered about three feet off the ground and faded fast into nothing once Joe noticed her.

This was enough; Joe made an appointment to see his doctor. After several tests, they could find no reason for his hallucinations. At the

Joe owned this business along Los Olas Boulevard. *Courtesy of Dorothy (Salvo) Davis.*

suggestion of his doctor, Joe decided to see a psychologist. After a few sessions, Joe still felt like he wasn't being helped.

One afternoon, Joe was surprised to see that his shrink had brought in a colleague to meet him. This man practiced hypnosis and was doing a study on past-life regression. He asked if he could put Joe under and told Joe that, if nothing else, this may uncover some hidden memories in Joe's mind. Joe agreed and lay back on the sofa, thinking this was the biggest waste of his time. After only a moment he was told to sit up. Did they change their mind and decide not to do the session? Both shrinks were staring at him funny.

"Joe, how do you feel?" one of them said.

He was confused. Looking at the clock, he saw it was an hour later! They had put him under. Next, they played the tape of the session, and he discovered that they indeed had begun to unlock the mystery of whom he was and who he had been.

After nearly six months of sessions, Joe learned that he had lived in southern Florida seventy years earlier. In fact, he had lived and ran a business in the same location where he just opened one. What is even more surprising is that he learned that the apparition of the woman he had seen fit the description of the wife he mentioned under hypnosis. Was she watching over him and waiting to be reunited with him? Strange how nothing weird had ever happened in his life until he lost his job.

One day during a session he believed he uncovered a reason for that. In his past life, he ran several businesses and was a cold-hearted employer. During the great Depression, he fired several employees, and those he kept he barely paid, knowing their desperate situations. He now believes he came back to learn lessons in this life he had made others suffer in his last.

Joe does believe that the locations he was at were haunted, but that he himself was once a villain of south Florida's past, and today he is reliving his past wrongs.

BEAUTIFUL GHOST APPEARS ALONG HIGHWAY 441

The couple walked around the corner of the plaza toward the Subway for a late dinner around 8:00 p.m. on a Tuesday night. As they held hands and flirted with each other, they were given a shock when a woman with an Afro walked out of the glass of the building and disappeared into a pillar on the plaza's walkway. This occurred on a winter night in November 1998; the plaza was located near U.S. Highway 441 and Oakland Park Boulevard in Fort Lauderdale. The plaza has several different kinds of businesses located there.

Marc worked at one of these businesses that winter when the sightings of the mysterious woman occurred. The couple on the way to Subway was the first encounter with the ghost he had heard about. He also heard that, later that same week one evening, many people saw a beautiful black lady in her twenties wearing eighties attire with a large Afro walk across a room and through a window to the outside. Eyewitness accounts said a cool breeze seemed to follow her.

On the same day, a lady using the restroom at the nearby license branch looked in the mirror to check her appearance when she saw the ghostly image standing behind her. She left the restroom in a frenzy demanding to be heard by employees about what she had just seen. The license branch workers threatened to give her a breathalyzer test if she did not calm down. They thought she was drunk and maybe a little crazy. The woman left outraged with the workers and fearful of the place.

Marc had thought all the talk of the beautiful ghost with an Afro was foolish until he had his own encounter. He was taking a break from his job and enjoying a cigarette when he felt a tap on his shoulder. Before he'd even turned around the hairs on the back of his neck were standing up. When he did turn, he came face to face with the rumored ghost. She was beautiful, he recalls. The woman had on a mid-thigh length checkered dress and chunky white heels. How he remembered this, he can't explain. Marc said the whole experience happened so fast, but he remembers it in slow motion. He remembers her having the most perfect shaped mouth and an Afro. She smiled and seemed to laugh at him, but there was no sound coming from her.

Then she seemed to dissolve into a mist disappearing into the night. With shaking hands, Marc dropped his cigarette and hurried back inside. As he shared his encounter with the others, he was aware of how crazy he sounded. He explains that when you encounter the paranormal it becomes a completely new level of reality.

There were several more claims of people spotting the beautiful ghostly lady over the week that followed, and then they stopped. Life seemed to return to normal at work but Marc could not forget what he had seen. Where did she come from and why did she make herself so known during that week?

After looking into reasons why she would have appeared there, a friend of Marc believed he found the answer. In the mid-eighties, a young woman had been walking down Highway 441 and was killed by a hit-and-run driver. Marc claims the accident had taken place exactly ten years earlier from the time people witnessed the ghost. No one was ever held accountable for the vehicular homicide. Perhaps she still searches for her killer and wants to make people aware she is gone but should not be forgotten.

The only thing Marc knows is that he quit smoking not long after his encounter. His reason was simple—he was too afraid to stand outside alone to smoke!

THE DEVIL'S TRIANGLE

One point of the Bermuda Triangle, aka Devil's Triangle, could be at Fort Lauderdale because of what happened on December 5, 1945.

On that day, the United States Navy was conducting training from Naval Air Station Fort Lauderdale. Lieutenant Charles Carroll Taylor was going to train his students about dead reckoning principles. Flying five TBF Avengers, the students were to negotiate a triangular course from Fort Lauderdale.

Flight 19 took off at 2 p.m. on a bright sunny day. At 3:45 p.m., the Fort Lauderdale tower received a message from the flight leader. "Cannot see land," he blurted. "We seem to be off course."

"What is your position?" the tower asked.

There were a few moments of silence. "We cannot be sure where we are," Lieutenant Taylor said. "Repeat, cannot see land."

Contact was then lost with the flight for about ten minutes. Instead of the flight leader, voices of the crews were heard: "We can't find west.

This TBF Avenger is much like those that were lost when Flight 19 disappeared in the Devil's Triangle. It was used as a trainer. *Courtesy of W.C. Madden*

Everything is wrong. We can't be sure of any direction. Everything looks strange, even the ocean." Another delay and then the tower operator learned to his surprise that the leader had handed over his command to another pilot for no apparent reason.

Twenty minutes later, the new leader calls the tower, his voice trembling and bordering on hysteria. "We can't tell where we are…everything is…can't make out anything. We think we may be about 225 miles northeast of base."

For a few moments the pilot rambles incoherently before uttering the last words ever heard from Flight 19: "It looks like we are entering white water…We're completely lost."

The navy sent a Mariner flying boat, carrying rescue equipment, to Flight 19's last estimated position. Ten minutes after takeoff, the PBM checked in with the tower but was never heard from again. United States Coast Guard and navy ships and aircraft combed the area for the six aircraft. They found a calm sea, clear skies, middling winds of up to 40 miles per hour and nothing else. For five days almost 250,000 square miles of the Atlantic Ocean and Gulf were searched. Yet not a flare was seen, not an oil slick, life raft or telltale piece of wreckage was ever found, according to a *Naval Aviation News* article.

A total of twenty-seven men were lost that day.

Finally, after an extensive Navy Board of Inquiry investigation is completed, the riddle remains intact. The board's report is summed up in one terse statement: "We are not able to even make a good guess as to what happened."

The other two points of the Devil's Triangle are Bermuda and Puerto Rico. Some say the other point is Miami, not Fort Lauderdale, but the misadventures of Flight 19 dictate otherwise.

The Battered Woman and the Mysterious Stranger

The side of her head throbbed and every breath she took sent a sharp pain down her left side. Lana Edwards was certain her ribs had been cracked again. The reflection staring back at her in the bathroom mirror was that of a battered and abused woman. Where was the beautiful five-foot-seven blonde woman with happy blue eyes and dimples that always seemed to light up her face? Lana's lean athletic frame used to hold her head up high as she walked down the street. After just two years of marriage, Lana found herself walking fast from each place she went, holding her head down and praying no one would notice her. By now, Lana decided that she had to find the courage to leave him.

Looking down at the broken glass vanity table Joe had thrown her into that morning, she knew if she didn't leave him soon that this marriage would literally kill her. Joe left for work and wasn't expected home for hours. Quickly stepping over the broken glass, Lana packed her things and left. That was the summer of 1989. This event would take Lana in the direction of a strong paranormal belief.

A few weeks after leaving her husband, Lana sat on her cousin's front porch enjoying her morning coffee. Stephanie had proved to be a perfect roommate for Lana during a time when she wanted to be alone with her thoughts. Stephanie worked the graveyard shift at North Broward Hospital in Fort Lauderdale and slept during most of the day. The situation gave Lana a lot of time to be alone. Lana felt she wasn't the best company to be around at this time and liked not having the pressure to make small talk. Over the last couple of years, Lana never opened up about the abuse she was going through. She was embarrassed and had kept her distance from her family. It had been over six months since she'd spoken to her parents.

After Lana left, Joe was angry at first and made several threats. When he calmed down, he tried winning her back by showing her a softer, more regretful man.

One day, she was reflecting on her life and the choices she needed to make when a man waved hello from the sidewalk. The morning sun seemed to illuminate the man, making his face impossible to see. It was late August in Pompano Beach and the humidity was high. The sun shined bright in a clear blue sky. "Having a good morning?" she heard the man say in a kind voice. Not wanting to make conversation, Lana just smiled and nodded. The man waved again as he continued on his walk. A moment later, Lana smelled old Avon men's cologne that her father used to wear. Knowing the smell must have come from the man who just had passed by, Lana suddenly felt better. Thinking of her dad, she went inside and made the long overdue phone call to her parents.

As Lana lay in bed that night, she realized that her day had been a good one; in fact, it had been the best day she'd had in some time. Talking to her parents and hearing their concern for her surprised Lana. She had expected to hear "I told you so" and not "We are proud of you." Just talking to them lifted a huge weight off her chest. She felt lighter as she drifted off to sleep that night.

The next morning, as she was preparing her coffee, the phone rang. It was Joe making the same promises of changing. When she refused to agree to come home just yet, his disposition changed. Joe became cruel, telling her she'd never make it without him. Joe lashed out, reminding her that she had no job and could not live off other people forever. She finally hung up on him after he told her she was too dumb to ever be hired for any kind of work. Lana was hurt by his words, but not torn apart as she normally would have been.

Another bright and beautiful sunny day was starting as she sat down with her coffee on the front porch. Lana was starting to consider her options and contemplate where she should look for work when she heard a voice.

"How is your morning going?" a man's voice called out.

Looking up Lana saw the same man that was there the day before. On this day, she could see him perfectly. The man was tall and thin with dark hair and olive skin. He was smiling at her with a perfect smile that she'd only ever seen on male models in the magazines. Lana guessed he was about ten years older than her, which made him in his mid-thirties. Looking at him, Lana nodded as she said, "OK, thanks." He smiled and started to walk away. As he did, Lana wondered where she had seen that jean jacket he was wearing before. It had a yellow and brown patch stitched on the left breast side.

When she was inside about an hour later looking through the *Sun-Sentinel* classifieds, it came to her. Before Lana had married Joe, her constant companion had been her best friend Josh. The two had been very close since their senior year of high school. After her marriage, they saw less and less of each other because of Joe's jealousy about their friendship. About three months after Lana was married, Joe gave her a beating, which convinced her it was not in her best interest to continue her friendship with Josh. Over time, Lana missed Josh but persuaded herself it was for the best that she no longer spoke to him. She had lost so many relationships with people she cared about because of Joe.

Putting down the newspaper, she picked up the phone and got in touch with Josh. He had no anger toward her. In fact, he was so thrilled that he told her that he would drive down from Orlando, where he was now living, to have lunch with her the next day. The rest of Lana's day went by great; she was in such an upbeat mood that when she applied for a job at a local Kmart that afternoon she got it! In the last two days, she got a job and connected with her loved ones again—things were starting to look up. That night, she found herself wondering about the man who passed by in the morning. She wondered who he was.

The next morning, Lana made her coffee and, despite the light sprinkling, decided to enjoy it outside. Flipping through a magazine, she was imagining how her reunion was going to go with Josh. She felt like a giddy schoolgirl. Lana was so excited to see her old friend; she wondered what she should wear.

A now familiar voice sounded, "How is your morning going?"

Looking up, Lana smiled and said, "I am having a great morning, thanks for asking. How is your morning going?"

The man smiled his perfect smile and said, "Perfect, just perfect." Lana thought she saw a twinkle in his eyes. He looked like a small child who had been caught well up to something.

The rain started to fall a little heavier and she asked, "Would you like to come under the porch?"

He just smiled and spoke with an almost a laugh, "My task is done and I must be on my way. You're going to keep having good mornings!" With that, he turned and started to walk away. Lana was about to wish him a good day when he vanished!

This startled her, of course, but she claims she did not feel fear. In fact, she was shocked by how calm she was, having just watched a man disappear before her eyes. She was still shaken up when Josh arrived at 12:30 that afternoon. Lana was so happy to see Josh! Not wanting him to think she had lost her mind, she decided to not mention what had occurred that morning. They hugged and immediately were lost in conversation trying to catch up. Lana realized that she was more comfortable around Josh than anyone else. During lunch, Josh mentioned having a hard time finding where Lana was staying. He said he got directions from a man who had the same jacket he used to have. He asked Lana if she remembered his old jean jacket that he had sewed a patch on. He thought it was strange the man had sewn the same patch on the same kind of jacket that he once had. This was when he noticed Lana had become perfectly still and was just staring at him.

When Lana spoke, it was with a shaky voice. She told Josh about the man she had seen the last few mornings and about him disappearing. Josh did not doubt her and suggested he stay the night and sit with her in the morning on the porch.

The next morning, coffees in hand, the pair sat on the porch having a great time in each other's company. Before they knew it, it was time for lunch. The man did not return; he was never seen again. However, Lana said he was right. She had many good mornings since she had last seen the mysterious man.

In the fall of 1989, she divorced Joe. By the following summer, she and Josh had married and they were expecting their first child. The years have been full of joy, and Lana often wonders if the stranger was sent to place her on the right path. Many times she has joked with Josh when he was leaving for work, "Don't worry about me. I got a strange man with a perfect smile watching me!"

Ghost Boy of North Broward Hospital

Gia worked at North Broward Hospital in Pompano Beach on Sample Road. This particular hospital was often very busy with the comings and goings of various people.

Her husband often came to collect her after a very long shift. One evening he commented that he had waved to Blair, her co-worker June's grandson, who occasionally visited his grandmother at work. Gia shared an office with June, but she was the only person left in the building. Her husband claimed the boy had been looking out the window of the room next to her office. When he waved, the boy responded with a smile and excited wave. The parking lot is well lit up in the evenings, and he claimed to have seen the boy very clearly and even watched him turn and walk away from the window after he waved hello.

Gia was puzzled and answered that, no, Blair wasn't there that night, but her hubby insisted that he had quite clearly seen a little boy with caramel-colored skin and a neat appearance looking in his direction from the room next to her office. He assumed the boy must have been Blair. Well, this window he referred to was in a section of the building that Gia knew to be locked. She had checked the door herself. The window was facing the parking lot and gave a perfect view from below.

Gia said they'd better go back because she assumed some kid was hiding in there and was now locked in.

Her hubby was shocked; he said the boy was very young and looked so much like Blair, who was four years old. They went back in and she shouted, asking if there was a kid in the stairwell. She and her husband came in to unlock the area. Sure enough, the door was locked. Gia unlocked the door and they entered the stairwell, which was deserted as it had been when she checked. The only other entrances were a door at the end of the hallway, where her office was located, which was always locked and only security held the key, and the other door led to the stationery medical cupboard that Gia had also checked and was locked.

She called security to come over and unlock the other door since they were concerned about the kid her husband insisted he'd seen. Inside was a small area, which only contained an old sink and the window Gia's hubby had been looking at, and it was empty—there was no boy there. They checked the other door, unlocked the stationery cupboard and checked inside it. The security guard confirmed that no boy had been seen by anyone in that particular area during the evening.

Gia's husband went to the window and stared down. Although a strong August lightening storm had begun outside, he could clearly see his parked car below. Gia's hubby was the biggest skeptic in the world until he saw that little boy. Twenty-one years later, he still believes that he saw a ghost and is still positive to this day of what he saw. That night made him a believer in the paranormal.

The security guard later admitted to Gia that, while doing nightly security checks, he had heard strange noises in that area in the evenings when he knew the building to be empty. In particular, that happened when he first started working at the hospital but he was too afraid to say that to anyone for fear of being made fun of. More interesting is that Blair did have a twin brother who died at birth in that very same hospital. Some physicians have made claims that small children will continue to grow on the other side. Could the boy Gia's husband witnessed be Blair's twin brother?

Another possibility is that Gia had investigated and learned that the particular corridor they were working in had once housed infectious-disease patients, some of whom lost their lives. Gia worked at North Broward Hospital for almost ten years after the incident and had experienced strange sounds and items being moved by unseen hands. However, never did she or anyone else hear or see the little boy her husband witnessed that August night.

THE HAUNTED KING CROMARTIE HOUSE

Another haunted house in Fort Lauderdale is known as the King Cromartie House.

The house was built in 1907 by Edwin T. King; he built the house on the south bank of the New River and it remained in the King family until 1968. King's daughter, Louise, and her husband, Bloxham Cromartie, resided there for most of their married life.

In 1971, the house was moved by the Junior League of Fort Lauderdale to its current site, where Smoker Park is now located. It was at this location where mass native remains were unearthed.

In 2000, some architects used the house to plan renovations to the old postal annex; they worked long hours. One night they made sure the place was locked up and set the alarm. As they left, they were startled when they saw an apparition of an old woman move aside the lace curtain in an upstairs bedroom window and peer down at them. She was said to have her hair up and pulled away from her hand and was wearing an old high-collar dress.

On another occasion, paranormal investigator John Carr and his team actually caught a curtain move aside on its own from a view they

This historical marker tells the history of the King Cromartie House in the background. It was first built in 1907 and is now haunted by an old woman. *Courtesy of W.C. Madden.*

had from outside in the parking lot. The video of this group can be seen on YouTube.

Now the house is used by the Fort Lauderdale Historical Society's research department.

Classic Haunted Apartment

One night while watching television, Joe Lopez could hear someone rifling through the files in his office. The sound was unmistakable: he could hear the file drawers open and then slam closed. Joe grabbed his 12-gauge shotgun and his brother, Ralph, picked up his 20-gauge, and they went upstairs, threatening to shoot whoever was there—but no one was there. Everything was in order except that a window was open. This was the middle of summer, and they were certain they didn't leave it open.

Joe Lopez lived at this address on Los Olas Boulevard. *Courtesy of Dorothy (Salvo) Davis.*

The air conditioning was running. They convinced themselves that the noise was just an animal on the roof, and that perhaps one of them did, absent-mindedly, leave the window open. This was the start of strange events at the apartment above their business on Las Olas Boulevard in Fort Lauderdale.

The second strange occurrence took place shortly thereafter. Joe had never been a good manager of money, and he had fallen short on cash with two days to go until payday from his brother. He decided to dip into his change jar instead of asking his brother for an advance. While dumping out the coins, he saw on the side of the glass jar what looked like a hole made from a bullet, BB or steel shot. It seemed impossible. Ralph helped him look around the wall near where the jar was placed, but there was no hole in the wall or windows. When looking at it again, he noticed that to make the indentation it did on the jar the shot had to come from inside of it. No human could fit into that jar, let alone bring a gun in with them to shoot a hole in Ralph's pickle jar piggy bank.

Several small, unexplained incidents like this took place over the next few months. Yes, it was somewhat unnerving but it felt harmless. The noises would always be upstairs in either Joe's office or the Ralph's bedroom. To rationalize it, they put it off as the building settling or some animal.

Then the knocks started. One night while he was working late, Joe heard an awfully loud pounding coming from the wall leading up the staircase. When he came upstairs to his home his eyes were wide open with fear. He asked if Ralph ever heard the knocking, and he had not. For the next few weeks, it was only Joe who could hear this knocking. And the more it knocked, the more fearful he got, and the more fearful he got, the more it knocked.

One day after a friend of Ralph's left the house, he heard a knock. He wondered who it could be at the door. They lived above a business but no one ever came up, and friends never just dropped by and visited. He thought perhaps it was his friend returning, but it would be odd that she would come back because she was late for an appointment. When he went to the door and peeked out, there was no one there. Just a moment after closing the door, he heard a pounding with urgency from the other side. Fearing there was someone else on the property, he went to look out the dining room window. When he turned to head that way, he was facing the wall near the entrance door when, out of nowhere, came a knock—then another and so on. The sound was steady like the beat of a drum. Ralph was so scared he could not move. His brain kept telling his feet to move, but they were like lead. He just stood there until this thing in the wall had its jolly old time scaring him half to death. Then it just stopped as suddenly as it had started.

They do not know where or how they ever got the nerve up, but when Joe came home, they went outside and into the attic to see if there were pipes under or around that wall that would make the knocking sound. There were none. That was the first and the last time Ralph heard that knock. Still, it liked Joe and would knock anytime he was alone. Their cousin Mike came down from New York to live with them and help out with the restaurant they operated. Ralph and Joe never told him about the goings-on in the apartment. They didn't want him to think he moved all the way from New York to live with a couple of nuts.

One night after a long day of work, Joe and Ralph came in around midnight and saw Mike sitting on the sofa with the television volume up very loud. It seemed he had heard the same noises coming out of Joe's office and the sound of footsteps walking or pacing just outside the entrance door. Whenever he pulled open the door there was no one to be found. Joe took one look at Mike and knew that Mike was filled with fear.

Mike is a biker. He is tall, with broad shoulders and about two hundred pounds of solid muscle. He is big and pretty much fearless, or so he thought. Ralph and Joe, who were both tall and thin, felt some satisfaction in their tough cousin being afraid.

Joe looked at Mike and said, "Did you hear something?"

"Yeah, I could hear someone on the stairs but when I went and looked there no one was there," Mike replied. "So I yelled down the stairs, 'You don't f--- with me and I won't f--- with you.'" He said that pretty much stopped all activity on the stairs. Then something started banging in the wall. He said he felt that whatever it was, it was pure evil. The more he told it to quit, the louder it got, so he just used the TV's volume to drown out the knocking. Joe and Mike were the only ones to ever hear the knocking again, but it would never happen until one or the other was alone.

One morning around 3 a.m., they were all awoken by the sound of someone running frantically through the apartment. It sounded like it ran right past both the east and north windows in Joe and Mike's bedrooms. Mike was a sound sleeper but heard the footsteps, too, and came running out of the room frantic! He thought it was either Joe or Ralph and there must be an emergency. He looked stunned to see both of them looking out the window at the sidewalk below. Joe and Mike went outside to see if they could find anything awry, but there were still no explanations of the sounds and no evidence of anyone lurking around.

Joe and Ralph's parents came to visit that next spring and things were still knocking and bumping around. Thankfully, due to lack of room, they stayed in a nearby hotel. Their father left his hearing aids at the hotel one morning when he had come to visit the restaurant. He went to the upstairs apartment to use the private restroom. Their parents knew of the ghosts and they doubted they believed them, but it didn't take long before the ghost made its presence known. While their dad was in the bathroom, their mom could hear footsteps crossing the room upstairs and his hearing aid screeching loudly, then softly, then nothing. Then it repeated until her husband came down. The restaurant had not opened for the day yet. It was easy to hear the noise coming from above when all below was still. Their dad couldn't hear too well without his hearing aids in, and so she asked him why he did not have the devices in. He said he forgot them at the hotel, but she was certain she had just heard them screeching.

Joe had about all he could take of the ghost when something else began to occur. Joe would awaken scared to death. He didn't know why, just that he was afraid, as if he was having nightmares but could never recall them. Each time he would awaken, he would feel someone sit next to him on the bed. Mike had since moved out and Joe was at his wits' end with all the haunting activity. The restaurant was holding its own, but they weren't getting along with their partners, so they decided to sell the restaurant.

Joe ended up going to the doctor because he thought he was going crazy. He told the doctor about the issues with the apartment, and he prescribed Joe some Valium to help him sleep. The doctor chalked it all up to the selling of the restaurant. He told Joe that he was having a nervous breakdown.

Then it was obvious Joe had seen and heard enough, and he moved to South Carolina. He would stay in the apartment about two weeks longer until the new owners of the restaurant were trained. Three days after Joe moved out, all hell broke loose in the apartment. The walls didn't knock nor did Joe's invisible friend sit on the bed, but there was a heck of a party going on upstairs. Ralph awoke not from sound but from sheer terror, like Joe had experienced several times before. He was scared. Ralph decided he would run out the door, jump in his car and get the heck out of there.

Then a thought came to Ralph, "What if they followed me? I would be alone on a road." So he lay there in his bed too scared to scream, too scared to cry, too scared to run. Yes, Ralph would be the stupid lady in the horror films who just stands there and lets the monster get her while everyone else in the movie theater is yelling, "Run, you idiot! Run!" He wanted to call someone to come be with him, but that thought was interrupted.

The apparition of a woman materialized before him, standing at the end of his bed. She spoke to Ralph without ever saying a word. She told him it would all be OK. He felt a peaceful calm come over him like he had never felt before or since. Ralph wasn't sure what he was seeing, so he looked closer. Ralph couldn't see her face. He wanted to keep his eyes on her; he didn't want to let her out of his sight because she was all that brought him comfort and sanity to what was chaotic and frightful. Yet he felt she wouldn't be there long, and he could only hope that the peaceful feeling was not temporary. She was transparent, but still he could tell she had skin the color of cinnamon and dark hair. She seemed to be wearing a fifties-era dress.

She reassured him several times things would be OK. He wanted to see for himself that what he was seeing was not a dream. He turned on the bedside lamp to see her better but she disappeared.

Ralph remained in the house for the rest of the two weeks without another incident. When he left, he prayed that he didn't bring any ghosts with him to his new home. This occurred almost twenty years ago. Joe and Ralph have never again experienced any paranormal events. However, Ralph has seen the apparition of the woman appear in his dreams a few times over the last two decades. Each time he dreamed of her was during a hard time in his life. Ironically, the dreams woke him up and gave him a feeling of calm. Over the years, both men always wondered, who were the spirits that haunted the old apartment on Las Olas? But never have they had the courage to seek the answer.

THE HAUNTED THEATER

Tara had worked at the Muvico movie theater in Fort Lauderdale for only a day before she heard from a co-worker her first ghost story connected with the place. Tara was being taught how to operate the register when the popcorn machine light started flickering. The girl teaching her the ropes just shrugged and said it was just the theater's ghost. Tara thought these were just silly stories. There were two separate incidents that convinced her that the cinema was indeed haunted.

On one occasion, during a very exciting moment in the movie playing, an older gentleman distinctly felt someone in the row behind him tapping him

Besides showing scary movies, the Muvico movie theater is known for having ghosts. *Courtesy of Dorothy (Salvo) Davis.*

on his shoulder; he thought it was someone telling him that he'd dropped his jacket. When he turned to look behind him, there was no one sitting anywhere near. He peeked over the chair to make sure it wasn't one of the many teens in the theater hiding and trying to scare him. There was no one there, and his friend sitting next to him was cozying up with his girlfriend, so there is no way he could have reached over to tap him on the opposite shoulder. After the tapping happened a few more times, he left the theater complaining on his way out to the management about what occurred.

Another time, in the middle of watching a different movie, a thirty-something woman had to go to the bathroom and could not wait. When she walked into the ladies room, she found that she was alone. All the stalls were open and unlocked. She went into a stall and after she flushed and was straightening her clothes, she heard a woman in heels walk into the bathroom and go into the stall next to her. She'd heard all the normal sounds of someone going to the bathroom. Just as she opened the stall door to go wash her hands, the toilet was flushed. Thinking that the other woman and she would be washing their hands at the same time, she looked over and realized that there was no one in that stall—the door was wide open. Nobody else was in the bathroom. Needless to say, she got out of there very quickly. Before returning to her movie, she stopped and shared her story with Tara and her co-workers. They told the woman not to be frightened, because the theater's ghost had never hurt anyone.

Tara had her own experiences with the ghost as well. She was working the concession stand one night when it happened. She and a co-worker were standing next to the soda fountain when, all of a sudden, it started to pour soda. However, there was no cup beneath it. It stopped as fast as it started. Another time, a medium tub of popcorn lifted off the counter and fell to the ground during a rush. Many saw the strange event and there was no reason for it. On another occasion, several people complained to employees during a movie that a shadow of a woman kept moving across the bottom of the screen. This was frustrating because it was not something that they knew how to resolve. Thankfully, the image never appeared again after the showing of that particular movie on that particular night. For the rest of the movie's running time, the shadow never appeared again. These were the only strange things Tara ever had with the paranormal. After she quit the AMC theater, she's never experienced anything else and hopes not to. Tara guarantees this is a true story.

The Muvico is located on Twenty-sixth Avenue in Fort Lauderdale. Who the unseen movie patrons are is anybody's guess.

The Muvico movie theater has ten theaters, and no one knows how many ghosts. *Courtesy of Dorothy (Salvo) Davis.*

THE HAUNTED NEW RIVER INN

The New River Inn, a historic site in Fort Lauderdale first built in 1905, is said to be haunted. The inn was used for the planning of the city and was in the first neighborhood of Fort Lauderdale. The inn stopped being used as a motel in the 1960s and became run down. That's when the Fort Lauderdale Historical Society stepped in and acquired it to restore and make it one of its own buildings. The New River Inn was added to the U.S. National Register of Historic Places on June 19, 1972.

The stately building is supposedly haunted by a small girl who plays hide-and-seek behind the trees out front; she's also been seen on the upper porch. The girl is said to be a former student of Miss Ivy Cromartie's first class in 1899. The young girl fits the description of LuLu Marshal, who was in that class. Why LuLu is haunting the inn is anyone's guess, but the class she attended wasn't at the inn.

The palm of a hand has been seen on the window on the front door of the New River Inn, which isn't new at all—it was built in 1905. *Courtesy of Dorothy (Salvo) Davis.*

The New River Inn now houses the main museum for the historical district of old Fort Lauderdale. *Courtesy of W.C. Madden.*

Another spirit claimed to be seen at the inn is that of Philemon Nathaniel Bryan, who was in his sixties when the inn was built, who died at age 85. Many people have claimed to see the face of the old man with a beard staring back at them—it could be his ghost. The palm of a hand has mysteriously appeared on the windows of the front door in some photos taken of it, too.

Another story is of the 1907 newlywed who waits at the New River Inn for her husband who never arrives. He never arrives because he was murdered in New York by the bride-to-be's angry father, who wanted her to become a nun. This story is told on the ghost tour held in Fort Lauderdale.

The New River Inn is now used as the main museum building for the Fort Lauderdale History Center. Events—weddings, bar mitzvahs, corporate events and the like—are held in the inn. It's also now part of the River Walk in Fort Lauderdale in the oldest part of the city.

You'll have to pay the place a visit to see for yourself if it's actually haunted.

THE VIXEN OF THE ELBO ROOM

He leaned in to hold her. She fit perfectly in his arms, and the sweet scent of strawberries from her shampoo overpowered his senses. Running his fingers through her waist-length blonde hair, Josh would have sworn in that moment he'd met the woman he would one day marry. Josh felt that particular night was so surreal for him, and it was about to get even more unbelievable.

Earlier that night, Josh's friend Steve had talked him into going to the Elbo Room on the Fort Lauderdale strip. Josh agreed and put on his favorite pair of bell-bottom jeans, as was the style, and slicked his dark brown hair back. Looking at his reflection before heading out, he liked what he saw: a five-foot, eleven-inch lean and trim young man with extreme blue eyes and a dimple in his left cheek. He thought of himself

The Elbo Room is a haunted restaurant in Fort Lauderdale. *Courtesy of Dorothy (Salvo) Davis.*

as a real ladies man. Always the lion and never the prey, he held all the cards in his world of single life. The year was 1976, and Josh was twenty-four years old and just looking for a good time.

Around 8:30 on a clear and warm April night, Josh and Steve arrived at the Elbo Room. The spring-break crowd had packed the ocean-front bar and there was a thrill in the air. The two men decided to grab a beer and hang out on the second-floor rooftop. "This was the perfect location to scope out the broads." Josh recollects. This was to be an average Friday night in Fort Lauderdale with beer and broads, no regrets and a whole lot of fun.

Before Josh could even set eyes on the lucky girl to be the mark, he became the prey. Before the hour was over, Josh would have a broken heart that would haunt him the rest of his life. Everything around him became still when he spotted her. A beauty like he'd never seen before, she had skin the color of warm honey and eyes as green as emeralds. Her waist-length blonde hair seemed to have a glow, and her smile was vibrant when she set her eyes on him.

The beauty in the sixties-style white party dress walked up to Josh and, without a word, put her hand in his and pulled him along. Instantly, he became like a puppy, eager to follow her and obey her every wish. She led him down the stairs and outside the open bar. Once they were outside, she faced Josh, took both his hands into hers and just stared into his eyes. He admits to having become numb all over and experiencing an intense feeling he'd never before felt. Josh knew he'd fallen under the beautiful vixen's spell. Before he could even ask her name, she stepped on her tiptoes and brought her lips to his. To this day, it was the most erotic kiss he'd ever received. Then she leaned her body into his and there they stood for the next five minutes just hugging. Josh glimpsed his future with this woman and felt at peace while taking in her essence.

When he was about to pull apart and look into her lovely face, he stumbled forward and landed hard on his knees! The beauty in his arms had completely disappeared! He got many strange looks as he sat on the sidewalk trying to wrap his mind around what just happened. He knew he was not drunk because he had not even had a chance to finish his first beer before the vixen took him away and put a hole in his heart before disappearing. Later, Steve remarked how stunning the woman was that had led Josh away and asked what happened. Josh was too confused with the truth to even answer Steve's simple question.

For the next few years, Josh frequented the Elbo Room, hoping to once again see the beautiful girl. He heard stories of others who spotted a beautiful woman in a white sixties-style party dress, but she always seemed to disappear before anyone reached her. Who this woman was may never be known.

Josh married and had a wonderful family, but he has never forgotten the few moments he held the most beautiful creature he'd ever seen. She left a void in his heart that has never healed.

Fort Lauderdale's Elbo Room has been a spring-break destination for travelers since 1938. It's a legend. The award winning movie *Where the Boys Are* was filmed there for spring break scenes in 1959. In 1998, the Elbo Room was one of the first places to open its doors to the world with online web cams and chat rooms that are still active today.

Elboroom.com allows viewers online to join the party through the patio or band cameras. Who knows, maybe the beauty in white will eventually be caught on camera, allowing the world a glimpse! Keep your eyes opened.

UFOs in Fort Lauderdale

Probably one of the first sightings of unidentified flying objects came in 1952 when there were reports of flying saucers over the skies of the northwest section of Fort Lauderdale. At the time, the United States Air Force was conducting Project Blue Book and sent an intelligence officer, Major William Frazier, to investigate the matter.

Three men were preparing to go to work about 6:45 a.m. on an August morning when they saw a "very bright light sparkling like a big mirror." The three men watched the discs for at least a minute, but they heard no sound.

The United States Air Force closed the book on Project Blue Book in 1969; the military concluded there had been no evidence of extraterrestrial vehicles.

However, others sightings have occurred since that time in the area. Clay Parker said he saw a large red object about three thousand feet away moving off the beach to the west at a slow speed for about four minutes, and then it shot straight up and vanished, according to My UFO Sightings Blog, myufo.com.

On Halloween night in 2000, Eli saw an unidentified light in the sky, according to UFO Sightings from Mystical Universe, a website, mysticaluniverse.com. "I looked up into the sky and for a split instant saw a shaft of light, which I think was some kind of narrow spray of electrons but that's just a theory," he wrote. "It wasn't very impressive, it was dim, milky, didn't change colors or directions, it was just a milky shaft of white light."

The latest sighting came in 2009 when Jack Scott and his friend saw an object crossing the wrong way over the runway at Fort Lauderdale airport with no lights and created no sound, according to UFO World News website, ufoworldnews.com.

The Haunted Samba Room

The Samba Room in Fort Lauderdale is said to be haunted. The famous restaurant is located on East Las Olas Boulevard in Fort Lauderdale and has an award-winning Latin cuisine. It also offers buffets and a swank custom menu.

The ghost of a girl with waist-length straight hair wearing a black skirt and a white top has been seen from the corners of the restaurant and then—just like that—disappears.

Napkins have levitated off the tables and glasses have cracked right before customers' eyes when no one is even holding them.

An undisclosed celebrity is said to have been startled when a hand forced him to remain in his seat when he tried to stand and nobody was nearby.

One night a woman was in the ladies room and claims to have heard a whistle before she felt a cold kiss on her cheek.

The staff claims there are cold drafts and phantom sounds after hours. They have become used to hearing odd stories.

You'll have to go there some time and have dinner to see for yourself.

The Samba Room is famous for its cuisine and ghosts. *Courtesy of Dorothy (Salvo) Davis.*

SOUL MATES REUNITED ALONG SHORE

The following paranormal encounter is not that of a location but a woman herself. Gina claimed to have an out-of-body experience when consciousness left her body. She claims to have been folding laundry at a local laundromat in Fort Lauderdale when she suddenly saw golden spots in front of her eyes. While looking down toward her feet on the floor, she was shocked to see she was elevated about six feet above a body that had apparently fainted. After several disbelieving moments, she realized it was her body she was staring at. At a time when her heart would normally have been pounding in her chest, she felt an unusual calm and wonder.

As she continued to look down in amazement, her name was suddenly called. The voice was so tender and familiar to her. Turning in the direction of her name, she saw a man. He was surrounded in a bright glow and only his waist and above could be seen. His hair was shaped perfectly around his handsome head and was thick and wavy. His cheekbones were well-defined in his perfectly darkened, olive complexioned face. Most notable to Gina was the intensity of his deep, almond-colored eyes surrounded by thick lashes. He looked at her directly with the confidence of knowing love existed between them.

This sign shows people where the shore is located in Fort Lauderdale. *Courtesy of Dorothy (Salvo) Davis.*

A scene appeared before her mind's eye and Gina saw the man as he was alive. In his arms was a beautiful woman with skin as dark as his and dark eyes glowing with joy. Pink lips formed a perfect smile on her lips as she gazed into his eyes. The man's hand ran down the woman's dark, thick waist-length hair and around her wide hips to rest on the swell of her expecting stomach. A feeling of euphoria consumed Gina, and she wished to remain a witness to the scene before her forever.

Then just as suddenly as the episode had started, Gina found herself returned to her body. A few people were helping her sit up and offering a cool drink. Later that evening, she sat with her mom in their small kitchen in Sunrise. Gina retold her out-of-body adventure. Her mother, a devote Irish-Catholic, found Gina's story hard to believe. Next, she revealed that she believed herself to be the dark beauty in a past life. In addition, Gina said that she loved the mysterious man in her vision.

Looking at her daughter with white blonde hair, glowing blue eyes and pale skin, Gina's mother became alarmed when she saw the sincerity on her daughter's face. Concerned, she took the then seventeen-year-old Gina to visit with their priest.

Over the next few weeks, Gina's family and the priest tried to convince her that she had experienced a hallucination brought on by the recent loss of her father. It became clear to Gina that she couldn't share her experiences with the man who had continued to haunt her dreams since her first magical introduction to her in the laundromat. That moment was like finding a purpose in this sometimes harsh and cruel world for Gina.

Over the next several years, she continued to dream of him. In fact, she became convinced he was her soul mate. The dreams would show them at different times. Most often, they were in Hawaii and dressed in period clothing to whatever time the dream took place in. On one occasion, she witnessed the death of her soul mate, whose name she believed to be Kalakuaa. They were standing together on a hillside near a cliff's edge. Her hands were bound, and a rope attached her to several more women. Kalakuaa was standing side by side with several other men. Shirtless men with sharp spears began to force the men over the edge into the harsh water below. When Kalakuaa was forced to jump, Gina sat up in bed screaming. Tears fell down her cheeks and her wrist throbbed. Looking at the palms of her hands, she had seen that she'd dug her own nails into them, making fists out of fear. This dream still haunted her nearly thirty years later.

Her family had all moved away from the South Florida area, but Gina remained alone. Over the last decade, Kalakuaa has appeared to her many times as she dreamed. Her favorite recollection of time spent with him was during the 1870s. Gina claimed that Kalakuaa was a crowned king of Hawaii and she his most prized and loved mistress. Their stolen moments together had been full of passion and lust for one another.

On another occasion, he visited her in her current life. Holding her hand and walking on the beach during the dream, he was tender and kind. He spoke to her, telling her she would find him again along the Fort Lauderdale shore. Like a puzzle yet to be solved, Gina waited alone for clues to this great mystery that has been with her. On any given evening,

The Fort Lauderdale Beach Boulevard takes tourists along the shore. *Courtesy of Dorothy (Salvo) Davis.*

you could find Gina sitting alone by the shore watching the sunset and waiting for her lover's return.

This would make a perfect ending to a romantic story. Sadly, Gina's story goes on. What you have read of this story so far was relayed by her niece, Stephanie. In 2007, Gina had a heart attack after coming home from one of her evenings on the beach. Her roommate found her the next morning on the living room floor holding a book of Hawaiian history clutched to her chest. Stephanie had come with her mom to help arrange Gina's funeral. Gina left in her will that she wanted to be cremated and her ashes spread out along the shore of Fort Lauderdale.

On the night of the funeral, Stephanie took a walk alone on the Fort Lauderdale beach. There were several people around, but she paid no attention to them; her thoughts were grieving for her deceased Aunt Gina. As she stopped and looked at the falling sun out along the sea, the waves splashed her ankles and her toes squished in the sand. A cold breeze blew past her, raising her long dark hair in the breeze. Her name was whispered into her ear so suddenly that the fear of it nearly knocked her five-foot, nine-inch thin frame into the sand.

Recovering her balance, her pitch black eyes widened in disbelief! Just above the water was the transparent form of her Aunt Gina. The apparition looked so sad and desperate. Then she spoke to Stephanie, "I can't find him! I can't find him!" Panic was the only word that came to Stephanie's mind when describing the sound of Gina's voice. The previous summer when visiting her Aunt Gina, she learned of her aunt's belief in her soul mate. The idea her aunt had not found Kalakuaa in death was almost too much to even bare.

About a month after leaving Florida, Stephanie learned that she was expecting her first child. At this point, Stephanie confesses she was an emotional wreck. Her aunt haunted her dreams. When she thought she could take no more, relief came in the form of an angel.

One October night, when she was two months pregnant, she was awoken from sleep. At the foot of her bed stood Gina with what appeared to be a dark masculine angel glowing softly beside her. Although her lips didn't move, Stephanie could hear words. The air was warm in the room despite the cold Colorado night outside. The sweet smell of lavender seemed to keep Stephanie's nerves at ease. A strange kind of humming came from the angelic being beside Gina that seemed to be for Stephanie's comfort. The angel said: "You will have twins, a boy and girl. Please name them Kalakuaa and Kaahumanu. We chose you to bring us back." As she accepted the message she was given, peace fell upon her soul. Then as if a magic wand had been tipped the images disappeared.

Stephanie's husband laughed at her wild pregnant imagination when she woke him and told him of what she'd just seen. Despite his laughter and lack of belief, he liked the names she gave him. He was from the island of Hawaii himself and thought the names were perfect if she did indeed have twins, which he doubted.

To everyone's shock and pleasure, Stephanie did indeed give birth to a healthy boy and girl with beautiful dark hair and almond eyes. Their skin was a gorgeous dark olive color. Kaahumanu and Kalakuaa have grown into wonderful toddlers who have a great sibling love for each other. A desire that Stephanie can't explain came over herself and her husband to move to south Florida. Today, the children love it when they are taken to the Fort Lauderdale beach to play in the sand. In fact, it seems to be their favorite place to visit and play.

Past lives are thought by many to be a paranormal phenomena brought on through hypnosis, astral projection and meditation. Why Gina's life was so affected by her belief, we cannot say. To simply close the story with her niece Stephanie's answer seems fit: "True and unconditional love found its way back to Gina."

The Haunted Stranahan House

The Stranahan House is a famous historical home in the heart of Fort Lauderdale and it may be haunted as well. At least that's what some have said about it.

The house was first built in 1901 by Frank Stranahan. Standing on the banks of the New River in downtown Fort Lauderdale, the house is one

The old Stranahan House, on the banks of the intercoastal waterway, is said to be haunted. *Courtesy of W.C. Madden.*

of the few structures still standing from the city's beginnings. Frank chose the site to operate a barge ferry across the river as part of the new road from Lantana to what now is North Miami.

Stranahan also operated a trading post nearby and traded with the Seminole Indians. He traded with them cooking utensils, ammunition and staples for alligator hides, otter skins, eggs and fresh vegetables.

Frank married another pioneer to the area, Ivy Julia Cromartie, the first school teacher in Fort Lauderdale. He married her and the house became their home. They entertained guests on the second floor for dances and community festivals.

During Ivy's free time, she taught the Seminole children. One morning a young Seminole girl had traveled several miles to the Stranahan home and was dehydrated by the time she arrived. She died at the bottom of the stairs in Ivy's arms.

During the Depression, Frank came down with a terminal illness and tried to commit suicide to end his life. He was finally successful one day. He tied a heavy weight to himself and jumped into the intercoastal waterway in his backyard. His brother tried in vain to save him but was unable to pull him back up. Today, an apparition of that event still occurs.

Ivy continued to live upstairs in the home and leased the first floor to a restaurant. Ivy lived a long life and died in 1971.

Two years later the house was named to the National Register of Historic Places. The restaurant closed in 1979 and the Fort Lauderdale Historic Society took possession.

Over the years, several people died in the home; Ivy's sister had several miscarriages there. When she finally made it to late pregnancy her husband went back up north to see to business. During a dinner party some guest from up north informed the poor girl her husband had another wife and children up there. This sent her into early labor. The baby was born stillborn in the upstairs bedroom. Afterward, Ivy's sister hid that she was still bleeding and purposely bled to death.

Ivy's brother-in-law had ties to Al Capone, who opened several brothels nearby. The brother-in-law was said to love the ladies. Some women have felt warm in the home, while men have felt cold, so perhaps women are more welcome in the structure then men.

The Stranahan House is now a museum, and it's haunted! *Courtesy of Dorothy (Salvo) Davis.*

Ivy's brother, Albert Cromartie, also died in the house. Tourists started taking tours of the home and some thought they heard voices. Some heard a man tell them to "Get out!" or some other smart aleck remark. That may have been Albert.

In any case, you'll have to take a tour of the structure to see for yourself if it's really haunted or not.

Florida's Strange Panther

Robert doesn't know exactly what he saw some time ago, but he considered it a very strange creature. It started as a black panther and ended up to be something else. In any case, it was different.

He said the incident happened during the middle of summer, not sure about the year—maybe 1988 or 1989. Anyway, he was doing some night fishing along a canal in Fort Lauderdale off the Dixie Highway. He and a friend were catching many turtles, which was odd but the water was so low—lowest he had ever seen it. They had decided to leave at around 3 in the morning and had to walk between a patch of trees and tall grass to get to the road where they had parked. They had a full-size cargo van,

Florida's black panther is rare and rarely seen by humans. *Courtesy of ClipArt 2.*

and the trees and shrubs brushed the mirrors on each side of the van as they drove through them.

As they were heading toward the main road, just through the small patch of trees, a huge black cat, maybe four feet long—not including the tail—came out of the right side of the trees. It jumped across directly in front of the van but somewhat higher than the headlights. Its tail was very thick and black with a rounded tip and very long. Then it disappeared in the left side of the trees.

This entire incident took place in a matter of seconds. They stopped the van and turned off the engine as they listened for any sounds in the nearby shrubs and grass. Then out of the corner of his left eye, Robert saw a shadow. Both men turned their eyes in the shadow's direction. This particular shadow was standing in front of the van but off to the side. The shadow was that of a silhouette of a man. The men stared with mouths agape and eyes wide open. The shadow began to walk directly in front of the van. When it seemed to be dead center in from of them, it changed form. Again, it was the shape of a black panther and bolted again into the tall grass. They sat still without speaking for a few minutes and then sped off toward home!

Years have passed and they never did see it again, although before they left, both men kept hearing dogs barking in the distance; they had fished there often and rarely heard the dogs barking. This was not a regular cat; its length, tail included, was the entire width of their full size Dodge van, from side to side. That was a very odd summer memory, indeed, for them.

THE RESTAURANT GHOST

For over a year and a half, Mario had worked as a bartender in a Fort Lauderdale restaurant gossiped about for its supernatural occurrences.

Employees had reported spectral voices, people appearing in photographs taken with mid-1900s attire and contractors fleeing in fright after ladders and tools were repositioned in their absence. A co-worker told him once of feeling a paralyzing cold draft and heavy weight on his body. Then it felt as if something passed right through him. Mario thought that perhaps his co-worker had imagined the whole thing. Others reported being slapped on the bottom or a tugging of their hair. Yet he had never experienced anything remotely paranormal, until his last night of employment.

Mario had announced his impending departure and was going through extreme emotional troubles, which in retrospect may have encouraged whatever forces that created his experience. Entering an order into the computer, he heard an unmistakable, distinct female voice calling his name, four times successively. Thinking it was the intercom on the phone next to the computer, he picked up the phone and answered, yet no one was there. He then glanced over to the host stand, expecting the hostess standing there. The host stand was unattended. Finally, he looked to the service bar and asked indignantly, "Who called my name?"

No one had. The voice was distorted—almost like phonograph quality; yet inside his head was an internally audible message from beyond. The hairs on the back of his neck raised and a shiver went down his spine.

Then a cold kiss touched his cheek and he raised his hand to his face. There was no explanation for what he felt. No one was nearby but he knew what he felt. Was this a goodbye kiss? To this day, he is disturbed and upset over that restaurant and won't go back—even to eat.

HAUNTED ROCK BAR

The first time that Marc noticed some strange happenings was about a week after he had started at the Rock Bar on A1A in Fort Lauderdale.

The evening was getting late and he was closing the restaurant for the night with a few other staff members. They heard something in the back of the restaurant when they were all about to leave. They thought maybe it was just the ice machine making a strange drumming sound—until they heard a pop like a balloon being hit with a pin and then the sound a champagne bottle makes when the cork pops out. Marc and another male co-worker inched their way toward the sound and heard it again. Marc picked up a light push broom and pushed open the door to the kitchen.

Some say the Rock Bar in Fort Lauderdale is haunted. *Courtesy of Dorothy (Salvo) Davis.*

All was still and not even the ice machine or refrigeration system could be heard. Then suddenly a black shadow rushed between Marc's feet and nearly scared him into a heart attack. Marc and his co-worker watched this black orb-like shadow rise up to the ceiling before disappearing into the wall. They ran back to the others and said it was time to get the hell out of there. No one even considered taking the time to tell the boss who was in the office and what they'd seen. He was on his own!

Over the next few weeks there seemed to be nothing out of the ordinary. Then one night a female customer walked into the restroom and found a tall, trim and handsome Hispanic man inside. She mentioned to him that he was in the ladies room, but he said nothing in return. She left the restroom and met a waitress right outside the bathroom door. She complained right away about the man inside the bathroom. She and the waitress entered the bathroom to find it empty—the man was gone! There was no way he could have left without the ladies seeing him.

This was not the only time the man was seen by customers. On another occasion, Marc had to calm a party that was sitting at the sidewalk patio. They claimed that they were insulted when their waiter walked up to the table and just stared at them for a full minute before just turning and walking away without a word. They described the waiter as a tall, trim and handsome Hispanic. There was no one working at the Rock Bar at that time that fit the description.

One morning staff arrived to find a large puddle of water by the front door. Puzzled, they had no idea where the spill had come from. Of course they cleaned it up but it mysteriously reappeared within the hour! Later that same week, the staff arrived to find what smelled like spilled peroxide all over the floor and an aspirin bottle spread all around in the sink in the ladies restroom. This was odd because the restroom had been cleaned the night before. The toilet paper rolls had been pulled out completely and spilled on the floor. The staff shut the door and searched the rest of the place, which seemed normal enough.

A few days later, at about 4 in the afternoon—the slow part of the day—Marc was in men's restroom cleaning when he heard a commotion in the front. He hurried to the front thinking there was a fight between several people taking place. He walked toward the patio area, and there were customers beginning to fill the tables in front. At the nearest table to the entrance was a man head to toe in soda. He looked over at the table and saw soda was everywhere! He rushed over to offer help but the three people were already standing to leave. They claimed their sodas just exploded on them. He apologized for the inconvenience and offered everyone a free margarita—which were known to be fantastic and the size of a fish bowl—but they declined! They could not leave fast enough. And what could Marc say? He had no explanation.

Later that very night, Marc had his very own encounter with the paranormal. Marc had cleaned up a mess and was sitting at the bar drinking Bacardi and Coke when he saw someone sitting in the corner at one of the tables. He stood up and said, "We are closed. How did you get in?"

The strange man didn't answer but stood up and walked toward the bar. This gave Marc that feeling of danger in the pit of his stomach and the hair on his arms stood up. Marc reached over toward the kitchen knives, which were kept on the underside of the counter for cutting drink garnishes, but when he looked back, the man was not solid anymore but more of a wisp of a shadow figure. As Marc watched, the closer he got, the more he continued to fade. By the time he reached Marc, the man had vanished. The room was left feeling at least ten degrees colder!

Marc had enough: the very next day he gave notice he would be searching for another job. Over the next week, things were calm, but on Marc's last day the Rock Bar's ghost must have wanted to say a goodbye. The radio kept going up and down in volume all day, and there were more spills and messes that day than any other day Marc had worked there. Needless to say, despite the great food the Rock Bar offers and fantastic scenery outside, this was not a job Marc would miss.

CHAPTER 2

DEERFIELD BEACH HAUNTS

JILTED BRIDE STILL WALKS DEERFIELD BEACH PIER

A few years ago Dianne's dream of marriage and family was rapidly approaching on October 31, Halloween. She would be marrying her longtime fiancé, Tom. Born in the early seventies to hippie parents in upstate New York, Dianne's life had been filled with sunshine, rainbows and the power of positive thinking. A Halloween wedding was not her ideal wedding, but the woman in her mid-twenties would do anything to call Tom her husband.

During childhood, her closest friend had been her cousin Lisa. Naturally, Lisa was her bridesmaid and had flown in from New York with her husband, Joe, for Dianne's wedding. The couple had visited Deerfield Beach many times since Dianne had moved south; both couples loved to fish and often got together for their favorite sport.

One evening, three days before the wedding, Lisa called Dianne and asked her to join the couple for some late-night fishing on the Deerfield Beach Pier. The block-long pier with a large gazebo on the end juts out in the ocean like a giant finger, and fishermen can fish there twenty-four hours a day so it's a favorite spot for many anglers. Dianne's soon-to-be husband couldn't come along because he drove a semi truck and was on his last delivery before their wedding and much anticipated honeymoon in the Tennessee Smoky Mountains.

The Deerfield Beach Pier juts out far into the Atlantic Ocean. *Courtesy of Dorothy (Salvo) Davis.*

Alone and stressed with thoughts of all she had yet to do for her special day, fishing and reminiscing with family seemed like a nice distraction. She fixed her long brown hair into the usual ponytail that she wore. Then she grabbed her favorite jean jacket—her first gift from Tom—with a large iron-on rose decorating the back and left to meet her family.

The night air was cool to a local Floridian and the sky was clear and bright with many stars illuminating the night sky. She paid the three dollars to fish at the entrance to the pier. Feeling vibrant and wide awake, Dianne had a bounce to her step as she started walking down the wooden, wide pier with benches on either side. Surprisingly, the pier seemed quiet for 10:30 p.m. with not as many people fishing as normal. A girl's flirtatious laughter caused Dianne, with a natural instinct, to turn her head in the direction of the sound. Stopping abruptly, Dianne stood with her mouth open, confronting the scene before her. Tom was leaning against the side rail of the pier with a vivacious blonde pressed against his chest. The couple was oblivious to those around them as they continued their passionate embrace.

Torturing herself, Dianne couldn't take her eyes away. Only when Tom happened to look in Dianne's direction for a moment, meeting Dianne's devastated expression, did the couple break apart. At that moment, Dianne dropped to her knees and let out an ear-piercing wail. She began to bawl uncontrollably, publicly mourning for her suddenly lost hopes, dreams and future with this man.

Dianne's family heard the commotion and came to her rescue, removing her from the spectacle her reaction had created. Dianne had come to Florida to go to college years earlier. On her second day of school she'd met Tom. He'd walked up to her, throwing his coat over her shoulders; she had not realized how cold the air conditioning could get indoors and sat shivering in her T-shirt and shorts before Tom appeared. The next day, he presented her with her now favorite jean jacket and asked her out. The two had become very close until the night she'd witness his deception.

All of Dianne's family still resided in the North. A couple weeks after catching Tom with another woman, she packed up and returned home to New York. Family and friends claimed she'd returned home with her head held high. Dianne claimed she was grateful to have learned of Tom's affair before vows were exchanged. However, her personality and appearance confirmed her devastation for the lost of her first love. Tom was her world, and she'd put all her faith in him. As the weeks passed, her family watched her wither away.

On a cold January morning, Dianne's mother knocked on her bedroom door hoping to get her up to help shovel the walkway. Snow had fallen overnight and the morning was gloomy. When Dianne didn't respond, her mother entered her room and confronted the worst moment of her life—her only daughter lay lifeless across the bed wearing her favorite jean jacket. She'd taken an overdose of her father's pain medicine. Dianne had ended her life trying to forever soothe her broken heart.

The October following Dianne's death, her cousin Lisa and Lisa's husband, Joe, revisited Deerfield Beach. While talking a late-night stroll along the Deerfield Beach Pier, the couple reflected back on their times spent with Dianne; they felt a deep sadness at her loss. On this night, the pier was busy with many people fishing and walking. Joe felt a cool breeze brush past him. Lisa's deceased cousin, seemly in the flesh, passed beside the couple and touched the flesh of Joe's arm. Lisa and Joe became glued to where they stood, unable to move.

They watched the back of Dianne's long brown ponytail and jean jacket move toward the end of the pier before disappearing. How much time had passed, they did not know. Suddenly, they became aware of a man's voice.

"You two going to make it?" he said.

Turning their heads, they saw an older man in his sixties approaching them.

Introducing himself as Carlos Perez, he offered the couple to sit down and have a drink. Lisa and Joe were still feeling dazed as they followed Carlos over to his fishing spot. Carlos handed them each a soda and told them that he'd seen the spirit of a woman pass by them. Carlos went on to say that he'd seen the spirit of that girl wearing the jacket several times over the last six months. He and a few other regular

Many tourists go to the Deerfield Beach Pier to view the ocean and fish. *Courtesy of Dorothy (Salvo) Davis.*

fishermen had spotted her several times between 10:30 p.m. and 11:00 p.m. in the evening.

Carlos was stunned when the couple not only claimed to know the girl but also showed him a picture of her. Revealing her tale of heartache that led to her death, Carlos now viewed this spirit differently. Dianne was no longer a thrilling conversational topic.

Carlos began to pray for Dianne's spirit that peace would find her in the afterlife. After meeting Dianne's cousins, Carlos saw Dianne only one more time. As always, she was in her jean jacket and walking toward the end of the pier. She seemed to be searching for someone as she looked in all directions. The feeling that accompanied this spirit was a deep sadness.

Could Dianne be looking for her lost love or forever punishing herself by returning to the scene of where Tom was caught betraying her?

Carlos decided knowing the personal story of this spirit was too much for him. He found another place to fish. Over the years, he has periodically heard talk of the scorned woman. Never will Carlos return to see if Dianne still walks the Deerfield Beach pier.

He claimed Dianne's pain felt as real and painful as a paper cut, leaving a sting when her spirit passed by.

The Vanishing Jogger

Isabella Lopez is a tall and trim woman in her late fifties. Her long and thick golden hair has never changed to white. To look at her at a glance, she would easily pass for thirty-something. This is a result of being a personal trainer since the 1980s. She has always been a perfectionist and admits to having a severe case of obsessive compulsive disorder (OCD). This disability, as she refers to her OCD, is the reason she believes she never married or had children.

Isabella has to finish everything she started and solve all problems she cannot understand. Often, this has caused her to get ill by overworking herself. Her friends are never surprised to hear she is taking on more projects than she can handle and have given up on telling her to relax. Isabella also believes her constant need to finish everything is why she has been so successful in life. She admits to being very independent and has lived alone ever since she moved to Florida from Mexico when she was nineteen years old. She claims to be afraid of nothing. In fact, she laughs when she makes a self-diagnosis. "I never got the fear gene!" she said.

This self-proclaimed fearless woman was tested early one morning in August 1988. She was jogging along the Deerfield Beach walkway around 7:30 in the morning. Wearing pink polyester running shorts with her favorite pair of neon pink leg warmers, she bobbed her head as she ran at a slow pace along the walkway. The day was going to be a hot one! Not a cloud dotted the sky and the humidity was thick in the air. Listening to the end of Michael Jackson's song, *Man in the Mirror*, as it began to fade on her headset radiophones, Isabella decided to take a short break.

With her hands above her head to allow oxygen into her lungs, she began catching her breath. She began to feel more relaxed and lowered her hands to rest on her knees. She looked up and her breath caught in her throat as she witnessed the most handsome man she'd ever seen stretching his legs against a sidewalk bench. The man was about fifteen feet from where Isabella stood staring. He had on cut-off jean shorts with no shirt on and shaggy shoulder-length blond hair. She describes this man as having a body that was molded like a statue of a Greek god. When he turned and looked in Isabella's direction, he made eye contact with her. She found herself lost in his eyes—the man's eyes were so blue they seemed to glow as if a light bulb were behind them.

Isabella was stunned stupid as she stared back at the man. When he suddenly smiled, a shiver went down her back. The man had extremely white teeth and two perfect dimples appeared on his perfectly sculpted face when he smiled. She was the most nervous she had ever been and her knees began to tremble as butterflies fluttered in her stomach. She was unaware of the pedestrians passing by when the man began to walk toward where she stood. At that moment, her biggest problem was what to do with her hands. Her body became foreign to her and, for the first time ever, she became uncomfortable in her own skin. This stranger was definitely physically intimidating to her.

Summoning the strength to make the connection with her brain to smile and say hello as he was approaching her, she realized her temple was braking out in a sweat. Just when the man was in front of her, Isabella inhaled a deep breath and said in a perky voice, "Hi there." The wind was nearly knocked out of her when the man just passed right through her body! She felt extreme cold that created a tingling numbness to her body. Blinking several times, she shook her head and glanced around her.

Looking behind her, it was oblivious to her that no one saw anything strange. Everything seemed normal. A man with a baby walked past her and smiled. A small group of senior citizen power walkers headed in her direction. So they would not push pass her, she moved to the sandy beach. She spun in a full circle and continued looking for the man who was not anywhere to be seen.

Wondering what had just happened she dropped on her bottom and sat on the sand for an hour or so just replaying the scene in her mind. Isabella says that she wasn't afraid but confused and shocked. She was convinced that the man had walked right through her; it wasn't her imagination and she would prove it. Later that afternoon, she was sitting in a McDonald's and telling her best friend, Jake, all about the vanishing man at Deerfield Beach. Jake had been her closest confidante since she'd moved to the Sunshine State and was her business partner. She shared everything with him, no matter how nuts it sounded.

In the 1980s, Isabella says the country was still very closed-minded. Jake—tall, lean and colorful in his clothing choices—was a very open gay man with a kind heart for his friends but a lot of pent up hostility for the rest of the world. He was also very eccentric and always game for anything. When Isabella suggested he go with her to Deerfield Beach the next day to try to catch the ghost on film, he was thrilled at the chance for some adventure.

Armed with a Polaroid camera the next morning, Isabella and Jake started to walk along the sidewalk at the beach. The plan was simple: Isabella would jog in front at a very slow pace and Jake would follow a few feet behind. When Isabella gave the signal, Jake would be ready to snap the photo. This particular morning was warm with threatening dark clouds in the sky. The rain started to fall after the pair had jogged up and down the sidewalk area a third time.

Frustrated but not ready to give up, the two went every morning rain or shine for the next six months. After awhile, they began to just jog for the company of each other, and, for Jake, he forgot about the ghost man. When they got a job offer from a fitness center in Sunrise, they moved

Deerfield Beach was named for the numerous deer in the area, but it also has some ghosts. *Courtesy of Dorothy (Salvo) Davis.*

from Deerfield to about thirty minutes south. Still, Isabella drove every morning to Deerfield Beach and continued to jog along the walkway, listing to her radiophones and keeping her eyes open for the ghost man who continued to puzzle her. Even though her friends voiced to her that she was crazy, she jogged at Deerfield Beach walkway. Despite knowing there was other nearby locations she could jog, Isabella believes she went to Deerfield Beach due to what she now realizes today may have been caused by her OCD.

When she found the thought of the ghost man creeping into her mind less and less as she jogged along the Deerfield Beach—almost two years after her first encounter—he appeared to her again. Ironically it was August 1990, almost two years to the day she had first seen him. This time she was jogging along and had closed her eyes for just a fraction of a second when she bumped right into him. The impact was so hard that she almost stumbled backward on to her bottom but he reached out and grabbed her arm. The contact with him was electrifying!

He was wearing the exact same cut-off shorts he had been wearing when she first seen him. He still had the same shaggy shoulder-length blond hair and killer smile. He was looking at her so intensely that she could not find her voice. Then, just like that, he winked at her and started to walk right past her. She turned around watching him walk away and noticed he was barefoot. He looked as real as anyone did and she began to think she had imagined the first time she thought he walked through her.

Maybe she was just so taken by his good looks that her nerves got the best of her. Could he have just walked on past her while she stood there, having a silly girlish breakdown caused by a good-looking guy?

She was just about to laugh at herself and thinking she couldn't wait to tell Jake when she noticed the man seem to fade into a mist and vanish! Her senses became seemly aware of everything going on around her in that moment. She knew at that point she'd no longer worry about her sanity—she'd seen a ghost!

For the next five years, Isabella continued to jog in Deerfield until a job offer took her to Miami. She never saw the ghost man again. Knowing she had solved the mystery about what she experienced, she no longer felt the need to search for him. Over the years that have followed, Isabella has discussed paranormal experiences with other people who had similar situations. Some have asked her if she ever wondered what terrible fate occurred to the man for him to remain at Deerfield Beach. He was obliviously a case of an intelligent haunting, considering he smiled and winked at Isabella. He'd also reached out and grabbed her. She can still feel his cold touch on her arm. Considering he is aware of his surroundings, is it possible he just loved the location at Deerfield Beach in life?

For Isabella, credibility among her peers that have had close encounters with the paranormal is the only answer she needs for now. Her final words about the topic are: "Ghosts exist and life goes on. If you don't believe it now, you will later when you have become what you thought wasn't real."

A Final Goodbye

Joe sat beside the lake at Quiet Waters Park in Deerfield Beach. It was the exact spot that he and his true love, Tricia, had been sitting the previous year together. As Joe reflected upon his memories, tears started to roll down his face. It was a special anniversary for them on this particular day in March.

Joe booked a table for two at the Cheesecake Factory, Joe and Tricia's favorite restaurant. They had spent the last two anniversary evenings there. In fact, it was where Joe had proposed to Tricia three years ago this day, right after leaving the lake at Quiet Waters Park. The park on South Powerline Road is known for an annual Renaissance Festival in February each year.

Joe mourned Tricia's loss intensely—to the point that it consumed his life. Why did Tricia have to die? Joe couldn't make sense of it. Why did God punish him so? These questions loomed in his head constantly.

Quiet Waters Park in Deerfield Beach is known for an annual Renaissance Festival in February each year. *Courtesy of Dorothy (Salvo) Davis.*

Tricia suffered from depression and when Joe lost his job last spring all hopes of leaving their small apartment, buying a home and starting a family had all but vanished. Joe was optimistic that things would get better, but Tricia could never shake the feeling of doubt from her imbalanced mind.

One summer night last May, they found Tricia's body floating in the pool at their apartment complex. She had taken an overdose of various over-the-counter medications. Additionally, the authorities said that the water in Tricia's lungs had played a significant part in her death. To make things even harder for Joe, when the autopsy came back, he found out she was almost four months pregnant. She had never told him before she died.

As Joe looked at the water rippling in the evening breeze, he found himself dwelling upon the ducks swimming effortlessly in front of him. He wished that one of them would just rise up out of the water and turn into Tricia, and, just for a few moments, he thought that it would really happen. Suddenly, he thought he heard Tricia whisper his name in his left ear. Joe could almost feel Tricia's long thick black hair brushing against his face; he could almost smell her perfume but, most of all, he really could feel their love stronger than ever before. Wow, he really was losing it!

Joe knew that Tricia was gone forever and that nothing could bring her back, not even a special anniversary evening celebrating their love at the Cheesecake Factory, but he still needed some kind of closure. His therapist assured him a ritual of saying goodbye would help start the healing process. It was as if Joe felt that he knew what had really happened to Tricia, but he just couldn't put his finger on why she stole their future together. He knew she was unhappy, but sadly the signs of just how much only became clear after her death.

It seemed like a long drive to him to the restaurant located in downtown Fort Lauderdale and the traffic made it even longer. Joe was determined to celebrate this special day, although alone—yet he felt Tricia would be close by.

The table was set per Joe's instruction, with one red rose in a lead vase in the middle of a secluded, window side table. Joe sat down and ordered a carafe of semisweet white wine, just as they had done, one year ago.

The waiter returned with the wine and hovered apprehensively, looking toward the front door of the restaurant. Joe didn't bother looking at the menu and ordered right away. The choices were exactly the same ones he and Tricia had made, although the waiter did not quite understand. He acknowledged the order with a bow of respect and made his way to the kitchen.

Joe carefully poured two glasses of wine and set one of them down to one side of Tricia's place setting. Then, he picked up his wine and made a toast to the both of them. As Joe raised his glass, his eyes caught the reflection of himself in the window and for a moment, he thought he saw Tricia raising her glass and looking at him.

When Joe looked away from the window, an odd feeling crept over him. The hairs on the back of his neck bristled and a strange coldness blew across his face like an icy breath. Joe turned toward the door and noticed that it was closed.

As Joe turned his head once more, he suddenly became aware of a presence. The presence seemed to be accompanied by a familiar feeling that carried an impression with it. Then, Joe felt something touch his free hand resting on the table. "Tricia?" Joe whispered.

Although Joe did not hear a reply, he knew in his heart and in his soul that his true love was by his side. Joe was filled with a happiness that words could not relate—but why? This question had been upon his lips and had been hanging heavy in his heart for almost a year.

The smell of Tricia's perfume seemed to linger in the air. Goosebumps raised on his flesh. He needed to steady himself and regain his composure. He stood and went to the restroom. When he returned to the table an older lady at the table beside him came over. "I'm sorry sir, but the lady dining with you asked me to let you know she loved you but had to go. She said to tell you goodbye."

Joe was stunned! He asked for a description of the lady who left this message and got an exact image of Tricia told to him. The older lady looked at him like he had lost his mind when he turned pale. He walked out of the restaurant before the meal and stopped at the front to pay his check.

As the evening wore on, he knew that Tricia was going to be with him forever, just as they had promised each other. He also realized that Tricia's mental illness was of no fault of her own and that God had forgiven her. Joe knew that they were soul mates. It was the best anniversary ever because he got closure: Tricia had said goodbye.

Sometimes, as in Joe's case, a location may have the presence of a spirit, but it is not the location itself that is haunted but the person there. Perhaps Tricia still visits the banks of the lake at Quiet Waters Park in Deerfield Beach or her favorite table at the Cheesecake Factory in Fort Lauderdale, remembering her happy times in life with Joe. Like Joe, she may be patiently waiting for the time when they can be reunited forever. Not all hauntings are terrifying; some are simply enchanting with the possibility of endless love.

Home has Dark Entity

On a friendly looking neighborhood street in Deerfield Beach exists a home with a past of emotional rage; the home is located on SW Twenty-eighth Terrace in the Waterford Homes community.

In 1987, a young family of six moved into the home. The family loved their new home with the open floor plan and in-ground pool. However, not long after moving in, the parents began to fight, often leaving their four daughters frightened. The tension in the home could be felt like static electricity. The home became a place full of negative emotion.

Could there have been a dark entity at work causing the tension and fights? Some paranormal experts believe this can happen so the entity can feed off the negative energy. As the years began to pass, the sisters became very close and supported each other in the sad home. Both their parents were good people and good parents but inside the home they were plagued with sadness and misery.

Things started to manifest a few years after moving in. The two older daughters would often hear their names called in a whisper when they were alone. Lights would occasionally go on and off by themselves. One Saturday afternoon, the sisters were home alone playing Nintendo in the living room. Suddenly a lone female moan filled the house and seemed to vibrate off the walls. The frightened sisters dropped everything and ran outside the sliding glass doors that were in the living room. Looking back, two of the girls saw an apparition of a lady in a white flowing gown glide past the living room. So full of fear were the sisters that several hours later their father arrived home to find them all outside afraid to go in!

Eventually the negative energy tore the family apart. The father was a very hard-working man, and despite losing a lot of what he worked for, he gave up his home and moved out. This divorce nearly killed his wife, who couldn't understand it was for the best. To seek comfort, she turned to dark magic. She began to practice Wicca and play the Ouija board daily. She would beg and plead for answers on whether her husband would ever return to her.

This opened the door to evil, which seemed to fill the home; dark shadows began to appear inside. Two of the daughters awoke on separate nights with a choking feeling of fear and dread that left them paralyzed in their bed for several minutes. The daughters woke several times to the feeling of someone in their rooms with them. They would even feel the bottom of their bed go down as if someone had sat down. Fighting and violence began to occur among everyone in the home. The police were called several times as a result of the mother's failing mental health.

Strange events plagued someone in the house almost daily. There were times when a man's voice could be heard on the answering machine. There was no man in the home at the time!

A man with a large dark trench coat dressed all in black with evil and cold eyes haunted one of the daughter's dreams. In the dream he would appear to be standing in the backyard looking into the home. So real was the feeling that this man would give off that the daughter would wake up in cold sweats. The house seemed to be consumed by darkness.

This was proven when, one by one, every family member that left the home found positive and happy lives outside the residence. Eventually the home was sold to new owners and whether or not the darkness remains is unknown. However, it is fair to say that such a dark negative energy creating such fierce fighting among the living had to have left an imprint.

There is a true tragedy connected to the neighborhood where the home is located. On the dead-end street right next to the home, a young girl was raped and murdered on a date. They had been parked on the dead end when the murder occurred.

This dead-end sign indicates the street where a murder occurred. *Courtesy of Dorothy (Salvo) Davis.*

Several of the neighbors reported seeing a young girl in their home with long blonde hair and wearing a denim jacket. The family on Twenty-eighth Terrace saw the girl a few times over the years. Once, the oldest daughter caught a glimpse of her in the mirror as the ghost was standing just behind her as she brushed her hair. Another time, another of the daughters woke to find her sitting at the bottom of her bed. The young girl has been seen in other homes in the neighborhood as well, so she didn't seem trapped in one place.

One of the neighbors up the block had an experience with the young girl one evening. She was sitting at her kitchen table reading a magazine when the hairs on the back of her neck stood on end. Turning she found the apparition of the young girl. She seemed to be attempting to read the magazine over the woman's shoulder! Although the woman claims she was frightened but did not feel threatened, she never sat alone at the kitchen table reading again!

CHAPTER 3

POMPANO BEACH HAUNTS

THE HAUNTED SHOE STORE

In the mid-1990s, Dianne DiSilvia worked at a shoe store located in the Pompano Square Mall in Pompano. At the time, the thought of the paranormal had not even entered her mind until her third day of work as a sales associate.

Dianne was a self-confessed overweight girl with very low self-esteem. She had chin-length brown hair and brown eyes and wore glasses. Despite her mother always telling her what a pretty face she had, her peers had often been cruel. In fact, she had not even had a boyfriend when she started this job at twenty-four years of age!

The first day at work she met her assistant manager, John. He was a very nice man with a personality that put someone at ease upon meeting him. Within the first few days of working with John, Dianne began to develop a crush on him. John was six feet tall, lean and trim with a well-defined face and the darkest green eyes Dianne had ever seen. All this added up to a man she thought she'd never have. Despite this, she did work well with him and found herself laughing at his many jokes.

On the third day on the job, John asked Dianne to get some shoes from the back. While she was in the back, she saw a shadow pass down one of the aisles. The shelves were stacked with shoes from floor to ceiling with very narrow walkways between the aisles. Suddenly, Dianne felt light-

A haunted shoe store is located in Pompano Square Mall in Pompano. *Courtesy of Dorothy (Salvo) Davis.*

headed and claustrophobic—something she had never been before. She got scared and ran up front without the shoes.

John was with a customer and when he turned and saw her empty-handed; she was shaking. He gave her a puzzled look. He went to the back without saying anything to Dianne and got the shoes himself. Dianne was afraid he would be very upset with her. After the customer left happy with her new pumps, John took Dianne by the elbow and led her to a chair. Gently, he asked her if she was well.

Although Dianne felt foolish, John had a presence about him that made her want to always tell him everything. She told him about the shadow of a person that passed by the storage area. John didn't laugh but instead assured her it was harmless. He claimed to have seen the shadow himself a few times.

Dianne was still nervous. Whenever she was alone in the back, she felt uncomfortable but continued with the job. As the time went on, she and John grew very close. One afternoon, John asked her to get a bite to eat with him after work. Dianne let her low self-esteem take over and she turned him down. Before leaving that day, the two were in the back putting shoes away. They were about to turn and leave when a cold draft seemed to flow through the room. Suddenly, Dianne felt a huge push on her back. She was shoved into John. He had to put his arms around her to keep her from falling and bringing him down with her.

This act seemed to break the ice and after the fright wore away—the two did have dinner that night. One thing led to another and, before Dianne knew it, they became a couple. She was so happy, and she eventually lost over fifty pounds! She retired her glasses for contacts and bought some new clothes. For the first time ever, she was very happy with herself.

One day before closing up the store, she was looking in the sales floor mirror. While looking at her reflection, she noticed a man standing behind her smiling for a brief second. Turning around fast, she saw no one was there!

Not sure why, but she was not afraid. Dianne continued to work at the store for two more years. During that time, strange events happened but she never felt like she was in danger. Other employees saw other strange things that seem to verify her experience. In a strange way, Dianne felt the entity was very caring to those around the store. She claims that this entity made a huge difference in her life and had a lasting effect.

Phantom at the Wyndham Resort

In the fall of 2008, Jill was visiting her friend Robin, who had come in from Kansas with her husband, at the Wyndham Resort in Pompano Beach. The friends were enjoying one of the last visits they'd be having for some time. Robin was expecting her first baby, a girl, in the spring.

Having been friends since they were nine years old, the two women were as close as sisters. Both Jill and Robin were twenty-nine years old now. Blonde, tall and thin was a description that fit them both. The day Robin's job took her to Pompano Beach eight months earlier had been difficult for them both. Whenever they were together now, they made the

The Wyndham Resort was the site of a baby's murder in 2007 and now is haunted by that child. *Courtesy of Dorothy (Salvo) Davis.*

most out of every day. They laughed and forgot all their worries as if they were sixteen again.

The day had been perfect! Jill and Robin had spent a relaxing day by the pool and then enjoyed a game of tennis. Sitting near the window in her beautifully decorated room, Jill looked toward the sky. Did the sky ever get this blue in Kansas? interrupted her thoughts, Robin suggested they look through some baby nursery catalogs. Their husbands had traveled to Lake Okeechobee to fish and wouldn't return until the next day. Robin would be staying the night in the hotel room with Jill.

For the next couple of hours, the conversation was filled with talk of the baby and things that needed to be done. Around 11:00 p.m., the women's long day had caught up with them. They were exhausted and decided it was time to turn in for the night. Not long after their heads hit the pillow, they were both sleeping soundly. As they slept, they had no idea what was lingering in their room, waiting to wake them up!

Around 4 in the morning, the sound of water running in the bathroom woke up Jill first. Looking beside her and seeing Robin still asleep, she began to feel uncomfortable. Suddenly, she heard a terrifying woman's moan come from the nearby bathroom. The sound seemed like someone was in a lot of pain. Sitting straight up in the bed, she felt her heart pounding in her chest. The saying "spine-tingling terror" made perfect sense to her in that moment. Before she could even react and wake Robin, the sound of a baby crying came from the bathroom!

This noise had Robin sitting up straight in bed in an instant beside Jill; the old friends grabbed hands and with wobbling knees stood up beside the bed. Barefoot as they both were, they noticed the change in the temperature within the room. The comfortable climate of the resort room now had a very real winter chill in the air. Staring at each other, they both knew without words that they had to look in the bathroom.

Gathering all their courage, they slowly crept toward the room where the sound of a baby's crying continued without relief. Just outside the door to the bathroom, they stopped. Still holding hands, they listened to the sound on the other side of the door. Robin, with trembling fingers, reached her hand out to the door that was only slightly open and gave it a push. When the door opened fully, revealing the bathroom completely, the crying stopped. Then without either of them reaching to turn on anything in the room, the light went on and off and the toilet flushed at the exact same time!

That was enough! Jill and Robin grabbed a few things and fled from the room in panic! They'd only stepped a few feet outside the door when a sudden voice stopped them in their tracks. The single word "here" sounded loud and clear and had a soft but direct order when spoken. The voice seemed as if it were spoken by someone standing next to them. The problem is that they were alone in the hallway. Again the disembodied voice said "Here." Looking toward the right end of the hallway, Jill screamed! The shadow of a woman pointing in the opposite direction of the girls appeared a few feet from where they stood shaking! The black mass of the shadow seemed to have had long hair, which gave the women the impression that it was feminine.

Acting on instinct, both women ran in the opposite direction of the shadow. When heading toward the nearest exit, neither woman cared of how ridiculous they may have appeared to the few people they'd passed. They made it outside to Robin's black Ford Explorer and got in.

Catching their breath, Robin was suddenly very afraid for her expecting friend. They'd both just shared the most frightening experience of their lives! Robin suggested Jill get checked out at the hospital. Jill refused and said she just wanted to get away from the resort.

For the rest of Jill's vacation, she stayed in Robin's tiny one-bedroom apartment with both their husbands. When their men returned, they thought the girls' story had to have been their imagination. Of course, Jill's husband didn't want to argue with her in her condition. He agreed to get their things and check out of the beautiful Wyndham Resort.

The rest of the vacation went by fast without any more talk of the girls' encounter with ghosts. Soon they were saying their goodbyes, and Jill and her husband returned to Kansas. In March, Jill gave birth to a beautiful healthy girl. She remembers that the delivery went very smoothly until she heard the first cries of her precious new baby. The sounds of those newborn cries reminded her of the early morning cries she'd heard in the resort with Robin.

Thankfully, all the joys and work of the new baby gave her enough distraction to not think more on that scary encounter. Things were going along smoothly until she spoke with Robin about a week after being home with the baby. She'd told Robin about the moment in the delivery room when she'd first heard her baby crying and the fear it caused her to relive briefly. Robin took in a deep breath and told her of a heartbreaking murder a co-worker relayed about right after Robin and Jill's experience in the resort. That murder took place a year before their encounter with the phantom baby.

On June 2, 2007, an eighteen-year-old woman by the name of Ashley Truitt murdered her new baby at the Wyndham Resort. Ashley was vacationing with her family and boyfriend at the resort and had hid her pregnancy to them all. At 4:30 a.m., she gave birth to a baby girl in the bathroom of her room. Using a paring knife from the kitchen, she cut the umbilical cord and stuck her newborn daughter in a plastic bag along with the bloody towels from the birthing. What she did next is horrific! Taking the baby, tied in the plastic bag, she left the room. She walked to the end of her hallway and threw the baby seventy-five feet down a trash chute! The innocent baby died on impact of the fall. When she returned to her room, she went to scrub the blood from her hands at the sink. The sound of the water woke her boyfriend. When he got up, he noticed a line of blood in the hallway. Ashley responded that she was on her period when he asked her what the blood was from. He believed her and they both returned to bed.

The next day, a maid found the bloody knife and many bloody items in the bathroom of Ashley's room. The resort contacted the police right away. After the police arrived, they found the deceased baby in the trash dumpster. This was a very emotional situation for all involved. Ashley was arrested and held without bail; she confessed to her crime. Her reason for hiding her pregnancy was that she didn't know who the baby's father was. She confessed to cheating on her boyfriend. The brutal crime shocked the community. This seemed unbelievable to those that knew the girl; she was described as quiet and hard working by her teachers in high school. Ashley Truitt was tried and was sentenced to thirteen years in prison and parole for four years following her release.

Jill felt her heart breaking for the murdered baby. She asked Robin why she hadn't told her this earlier. Robin simply said she didn't want to upset her while she was pregnant. Both women wondered if the tragic event created an imprint of the crying baby. After all, Ashley was still living and they had heard a phantom woman's moan in the bathroom before the crying started. They felt this had to be a residual haunting from the desperate emotion being felt at the time of the crime.

Jill and Robin didn't believe that the baby would be lingering at the hotel. She certainly would have been taken to heaven on the wings of an angel. Still they couldn't explain the disembodied voice they'd heard or the shadow woman they witnessed. To this day and for the rest of their lives, both women will pray for Ashley Truitt and her daughter.

THE SUPERNATURAL DANCE AT BLANCHE ELY HIGH SCHOOL

Stephanie had long been a girl with her foot in the doorway of the sixth sense. Having seen spirits and ghosts since a little girl, she had a hard time distinguishing one soul from the next, often confusing those alive and dead. Due to this overwhelming dilemma, it was obvious that her social life suffered greatly; after sixteen long years she was without a friend, let alone a boyfriend. Despite being the late 1970s, the modern world still didn't accept seeing spirits as a normal ability, and it left those that did often labeled with cruel names, like freak.

Life as usual consisted of the same thing over and over, regardless of how the years went by for Stephanie. Get up in the morning with the same routine, go to school for the day, hope not to get picked on and go unnoticed at lunch, then come home and do what she needed to for class and her parents. Often she found company in the souls of the recently deceased, and they served as her friends until their regrets had dissipated enough for them to move on. As such, she was never truly alone, but being knowledgeable of her classmates or living peers wasn't her forte. However, with the coming of Valentine's Day just a few days away, she had the strongest desire ever just to celebrate the holiday with a living soul.

Flowers and chocolates aside, she thought she would be content with just a dance at their Valentine's Day Dance hosted by her high school. In preparation, she thought it may be best to approach someone beforehand to test the waters or even set up a date. However, since holidays were natural magnets to all souls, it became more of a chore to sift through the candidates of living first, let alone asking anyone.

Apparently the spacey look served to only creep out guys despite her moderate attractiveness, and she was avoided even further. With no other choice, she decided that her best attempt would have to wait until the moment itself.

Finally the big night had arrived! Sparing no expense, she got into her best battle form she could, dolled up with makeup, hair treatments, her dress and the works—she was set. All that was needed was to get there and win someone over! Equally excited were her parents, both of whom chose to escort her to the school on that cold but happy night. Stephanie just hoped it would stay happy, breathing one last nervous sigh into the cloudless starry sky before the cold creeping through her coat forced her into the car.

At last calmed down, she lazily watched the darkened trees through the car window as they quickly passed by. The unusually cold Florida February night could be felt through her coat as Stephanie exited the car. She let out a prepared sigh, she closed her eyes and, before she anticipated her arrival, she was there. It was a faster trip than she thought it would be, most likely due to the nerves and her eager anticipation. She could not even remember walking through the parking lot. Wow, she was indeed nervous. Quickly, she checked her coat and proceeded inside the gymnasium-turned-dance floor. Just as usual, it seemed that no one acknowledged her presence despite her getup. A bit annoyed, although still expected, she made her way through the crowds and to the seating area to size up her targets.

She was impressed. It seemed like a much larger turnout than the year before. In fact, there were many faces she didn't recognize at all, surprising to think that there were that many spirits drawn there. She shrugged it off. Tonight was her chance to dance with the living, not the dead. Without being picky, she decided the first face was the best, making her way over to a reasonably handsome boy sitting apart from the others. Summoning her strength, she posed the question: "E…excu…um… excuse me?" She was failing miserably! She kicked herself mentally. They weren't going to take her seriously like that.

"E-excuse me! Would you like to dance?" She said forcibly. She did it! Now the response—was nothing. He was ignoring her? Before she could say anything else, the boy sighed, stood up and walked away. She had failed after all. Had her reputation preceded her on such a scale?

Not to be discouraged, she tried on another. Ignored again. She tried to ask a less attractive guy and he went off with his friends without so much as looking at her! She tried smiling at others but they left her alone. Finally after several more attempts, she went to the benches and sat down. She didn't want to cry, but she didn't know what to do! Why was everyone being so mean to her? What's more, no one was even choosing to sit on the same bench as her. Were they that embarrassed to be near her?

After thirty minutes she began to wonder if it was best to go home. Even now, it didn't matter that she spent an hour on her makeup and it was already ruined by her tears. And then she felt it, something soft and gentle creep across her skin—like that of a ghost of extra potency. She looked up and saw an older boy, possibly seventeen, offering his hand to her. She didn't want to dance with a ghost, and didn't really care but regarded him anyways. He was definitely attractive in more than just looks, but what if he was there just to make fun?

"I'm sorry," he said softly, "but as you're one of the prettiest here, I just couldn't help myself from coming over. Would you like to dance?" Looking down slightly, his eyes were serious.

Without thinking it through further, she put her hand in his and got to her feet.

"I'm Daniel." He said softly with a warm voice. "May I ask your name?"

"Stephanie, my name is Stephanie." She said timidly.

"Then Stephanie, please honor me with a dance." He said again with a very out of place half-bow.

She smiled despite herself. "OK."

He smiled again and led the dance. As a matter of circumstance, the music in the background favored a rhythm compatible with a waltz and so they danced it, earning some very strange stares from the people around them. Stephanie could just imagine what it looked like, a girl dancing with the air, but she didn't care. For the first time in forever—she was happy. During the dance she was oblivious to everyone around them and that was fine. But after the first dance and the different ones to follow, Stephanie finally felt a weight lift from her heart. When both were finally tired from their dance, he led them off the dance floor and toward the benches. But rather than sit, she was surprised that he led her back into the entrance hall outside the gymnasium.

Ah—she understood. Now that he had realized his pleasures, he was going to tell her about his time in life. She smiled knowingly. He had helped her and now it was time for her to help him lose his regrets. "Daniel," She started, "I—"

"Stephanie," He said abruptly, cutting her words off, "I need to show you something. Because I need you to understand."

She smiled sadly. She knew it. "OK."

Daniel led her to the events bulletin of the news wall. Behind a panel of glass was a series of newspaper clippings of different events. Among them were sports clippings and school awards, but one seemed to leap out more than the others. In Memory Of—it was this one. Silently she let her eyes flit down the clipping, "Deadly Crash, No Survivors." She read out loud; how horrible. There was even a picture of a car flipped over on its roof, down in a canal. How terrible it was, to happen to a whole family and in—she swallowed. That car, it looked familiar; it looked—like her family's car!

Mouth open, Stephanie took a step back, mouthing a silent no in disbelief. Suddenly, she felt cold, her hair was wet and her coat was on her. She shook her head as her skin seemed to lose color and her breath could be seen in the air, her lips felt numb and her teeth chattered as though she had just emerged from cold water. She stepped back again and looked toward Daniel, who was wearing a very sad expression on his face. It wasn't possible!

She closed her eyes in an attempt to block the sight and seemed to be looking backward in time. She was sitting in the back car seat and looking out the window at the snowy forest beyond the window. That past image of herself sighed and closed her eyes, just before a cry of alarm caused them to open again just before a cascade of random visual and audio segments—an animal, screams, swerving, blackness, rolling, jumbled noise, interchanging bits of blackness and random images before an eerie silence. At last, a broken windshield could be seen and the slumped and unmoving forms of her parents, all of whom were upside down, before a liquid cold moved through the broken windows and bubbled up around her. The feeling of her fingers upon the jammed seat belt buckle and the desperation to survive the terror that had surrounded her entered her nose and mouth and the eventual embrace of eternal blackness.

When she opened her eyes again, she found herself to be outside the school, near where she had started this night. Daniel was just emerging from the building, apparently following her supernatural energies. She smiled sadly as she slowly came to grip on her reality. She had been like him once.

"It's been more than several years," started Daniel, to her back, "since your accident."

She held her eyes to the same kind of starry sky she had seen those years ago. "I think that your soul waited until this holiday, and until you found someone like you were in life," he said.

He put his hand in hers and she turned to face him. "I do know how you feel, and despite alive or deceased, I'm glad that it was you who were here with me tonight."

Stephanie smiled despite everything and felt the after effects of her parting moments begin to disappear from her body, reverting her to the state she was before ever knowing. "Thank you," she breathed, a warm tingling sensation creeping through her being as her body started to lose substance. "Really thank you!"

"Happy Valentine's Day," Daniel said to her with a smile as she began to dissipate into the air with a faded golden light embracing her. Her parents faintly appeared behind her. She smiled one last time before finally disappearing completely, her tears leaving a slight glittering trail that accompanied her ascending. All feeling from her hand in his disappeared completely as his smiling face whispered the conclusion of his sentence. "My Valentine."

This story was found in a journal Daniel had written about his paranormal encounters by his mother after his death in the mid-nineties. Daniel attended Blanche Ely High located at 1201 Sixth Avenue in Pompano Beach. Throughout his journal, Daniel mentions eleven different lost souls he'd encountered at Ely High. Stephanie is the only one he refers to as having moved on. He even mentions having an encounter with a very beautiful African American woman dressed in a fifties dress, intelligently demanding freedom for her civil rights. This particular spirit is interesting as the school is named after the very successful Blanche Ely, an African American woman. She was the only female secondary principal in the state of Florida until the 1970s. Could her spirit still be keeping watch that her work in life is being honored even after her death? Students of Ely High, mind your behavior, or you may not only have your living principal to answer to!

Ghost along Federal Highway U.S. 1

One late night in the summer of 2001, Mr. and Mrs. Perez left a friend's home in Fort Lauderdale. It was a Friday night about midnight; rain was coming down in black sheets. They were coming down Federal Highway U.S. 1 toward the Pompano Mall when the couple spotted a girl walking on the side of the road. They passed her by but their conscience got to them. After all, it was late at night, raining and chilly. So they turned around at a gas station and went back to ask the girl if she needed some help.

They stopped across the street from where she was. The girl was young, maybe sixteen, pale and tired looking with dark hair and thin frame. They calmly asked her, "Do you need a ride?"

The ghost of a girl has been spotted along U.S. 1 in Pompano. *Courtesy of Dorothy (Salvo) Davis.*

"Yes, I'm going to the movie theater by the Pompano Mall, just down the road," she replied. She rubbed her neck as she spoke; Mr. Perez noticed it was bruised.

Taking pity Mr. Perez said, "OK. Let me turn my truck back around and I will be right back."

She didn't say a word. She just nodded yes. Mr. Perez turned the truck around in the closest driveway. He was not so far out of site that he could not see the girl. As he backed up, he caught a glimpse of her staring at the truck as the rain poured down on her. They started back in her direction and stopped right where they left her. She was gone!

While Mr. Perez was turning around, there were no other vehicles that passed—none whatsoever—so she could not have gotten a ride with someone else. They called out to her and no one answered. They went back to the driveway, turned around again and went back just to make sure. They repeated this two times and, still, no one could be seen! Mrs. Perez, who remained speechless throughout the whole ordeal, looked at her husband and said, "Honey, I believe you were talking to a ghost."

He replied, "Well, at least you saw her, too."

A week or so passed, and they were at their friend's house again. They told them what happened and described the girl.

The friend's face got pale and he simply said, "You stopped to pick up a ghost?" He went on to tell them about a local high school girl who was going to meet friends at the movie theater on a Friday night but never showed up. No one saw her until a few days later. She was found murdered along the side of Federal Highway U.S. 1!

Mr. Perez's mother works at the Pompano Mall with several ladies who live in that area and are familiar with the story. They verified that several people have stopped to pick up the girl and she simply disappears.

Mr. and Mrs. Perez believe they saw that girl for a reason, like she was trying to tell them something. They just wish they knew how to help her find peace. They feel like she will haunt that stretch of highway until her murder is solved!

CHAPTER 4

CORAL SPRINGS HAUNTS

THE GHOSTS OF CORAL SPRINGS MEDICAL CENTER

For five years, Jamie worked the swing shift in the housekeeping department at Coral Springs Medical Center in Coral Springs. Jamie claims there are several ghosts in the building. Her ghost tales are amusing to her now, but they weren't at the time they occurred. Jamie was a floor tech; in other words, she cleaned and buffed floors and cleaned carpets.

One evening, Jamie was sent to do a room in Cardiac Care. As she went about her job mopping the floor in preparation for buffing, she noticed a heart monitor in the corner that was beeping. That monitor wasn't hooked up; when a heart monitor is left unattended, it will beep—but only as a signal that it's been left on. This monitor, however, was beeping in a normal rhythm: "beep-beep…beep-beep…beep-beep." As she worked, it started to give her the creeps. She went to the nurse's station, telling a nurse about it and how the sound was creeping her out. The nurse only smiled and came in to remove the monitor. She explained that heart monitors are not normally left unattended in that particular room. It seems that they have an odd tendency to come on by themselves, even if unplugged. That particular room's floor got only a cursory job that night.

Jamie had another experience in the Cardiac Cauterization Lab. Now, the cath lab area was cold and uninviting as it was without any paranormal occurrences. Jamie went down one evening to do the cath lab floor and found the area locked up; everyone had gone home for the night. No problem—she had a key. She went in, started moving stuff around and mopping as she usually did. Jamie noticed some dust in a corner behind a heavy shelf and got a vacuum cleaner with attachments to suck it out. As she was bent over, trying to get at the dust, out of the corner of her eye she noticed something that resembled a human form moving behind her. Jamie stood up and looked around, thinking a nurse or doctor had come in. There were always emergency cauterizations being done, and if that were the case she'd have to leave. No one was visible, however. Jamie even shut off the vacuum and called out but no one answered. Therefore, with an eerie feeling, she went back to work. A few minutes later she was putting the vacuum away when she was startled by the distinct sound of a ladies sigh. Looking around and calling out again, she found no one there. Goosebumps rose on her flesh and she immediately prepared to leave the area.

A few seconds later, right before she left the room, she saw something in another glimpse out of the corner of her eye. This time she'd turned fast enough to see the shadow of a person walk past slowly. A cold breeze seemed to follow and, on shaky knees, Jamie left the area fast!

Once in the emergency-room floor, she was working and saw one of the bed tables move, just a bit. She thought little of it, though. The tables were on wheels and would often shift when moved around, as she had done with them. Several minutes went by. As Jamie went about mopping the back of a room, she bent over to move a chair, and, at that moment, something slapped her hard right on the backside! Again, she was the only one in the area!

She knew that there was supposedly a ghost in the emergency-room area. The eerie events were seen by the nursing staff there and by one of her fellow housekeepers, the woman who cleaned the ER rooms every night. Many were used to the spirit—if that can be believed. How can anyone get used to being spooked?

The ghost was supposedly playful; a younger woman in a pink gown appeared most often in the ER for some reason. She could also often be seen walking alone in the Core area, the large surgical supply room that opens into all the operating rooms. Jamie thought that the good lady considered the cath lab as part of her domain as well. Perhaps Jamie was irritated a little for not paying enough attention to her antics—which may be why she often fell victim to frightful moments while working.

Jamie also had another little run-in with the ER ghost herself on another night. She'd volunteered to work a double to cover for the guy who usually worked the night shift as a housekeeper. At about 2 in the morning, she was called to clean up ER 6 after an emergency stitching. She didn't like that idea because she knew it was haunted. She also knew the whole area would be empty by the time she got there—and it was. Jamie got the housekeeping cart set up and went to the open door; they had graciously left the light on for her. The floor was spattered here and there with splotches of congealed blood and various disposable items used in stitching a deep cut were left lying around. Jamie, of course, had to wipe everything down and thoroughly mop the floor with disinfectant. She put on her headphones and the music blared. This was usually frowned upon but she needed the distraction. She turned her Walkman to an oldies station and started singing loudly along. Her eyes kept wandering to the chair in the corner where the housekeeper she'd mentioned earlier—who usually cleaned in the ER—often saw the woman sitting and staring at her. Thankfully, Jamie saw nothing. Playful ghost or not, she probably would have ended up cleaning her underwear out as well if she'd seen her. She finished up, put everything away and then hit the lights, plunging the whole area into darkness. The only light came from a dim light way up at the corner of the room in ER 6.

She walked into the ER and, suddenly, as she reached the middle of the hallway, the strains of *Over the Rainbow* thundered out of the darkness that surrounded her. An apparently disembodied voice was struggling to be heard as it sang the dreamy song! Jamie swallowed hard and high tailed it out of the ER, her feet barely touching the floor, hoping there'd be no more ER cleanups in that room until the next shift came on at 7 in the morning. There weren't.

There were other restless spirits in the hospital. Another housekeeper friend had to go up to Psych to clean a room. When she arrived and started cleaning, the nurse at the desk called her out.

"Look here," he said, pointing at the television monitor (there are televisions in each room, left on all the time, occupied or not). There, on the monitor, was a sheer cloud hovering over the table she'd been cleaning.

They rose and went to look in the room but, of course, saw nothing except that several of the bottles she'd brought with her had been moved. The guy said that they often had trouble with patients in this room seeing odd things or hearing voices—but then this was the Psych Ward, and such stories were usually dismissed. Maybe the patients aren't so crazy after all.

Some other odd things at that hospital have occurred over the years. The Whistler was a guy in work boots, jeans and a flannel shirt that hung out in the laundry. Staff often speculated that maybe he was an employee of the city who passed away on the job. He didn't come around often. He was usually heralded by a faint whistling.

There was a voice in the Morgue that was actually recorded once on a security guard's tape recorder. Over the whispery sound of the vents and faint machinery of the Boiler Room down the hall, a voice could be heard saying "Help" several times. Jamie heard that tape and says it was very, very creepy. It was no fake; either the guy was an actor of the caliber of Laurence Olivier or he was really freaked out by it, too. After that, he refused to go in the Morgue alone and eventually quit.

Jamie herself eventually took a job at another hospital. After time, she realized that she had to be honest with herself. If you don't want to be spooked when working, then avoid employment at hospitals. She claims that she worked at the other hospital for only a few months before taking a ghost-free job at a nearby school. Hospitals are sadly full of life and death, making these locations hot spots for the paranormal.

The Haunted Blockbuster

A Blockbuster in Coral Springs is said to be haunted, according to a former employee who wishes not to be named.

She was nearly fired after being accused of not locking up and turning off the lights one night when she would swear on a stack of Bibles that she did that before she left. She also said the backroom would be a mess sometimes after it was cleaned up. And videotapes and DVDs had been rearranged after being organized. Televisions would also go on and off by themselves.

Employees have also seen a little boy in the backroom, according to the website Haunted Florida, hauntedflorida.com.

It's also rumored that it has a ghost around Halloween time. For sure, it has lots of scary movies, like *Shutter Island.*

CHAPTER 5

SUNRISE HAUNTS

FLORIDA NIGHTTIME APPARITION

Lindsey Harris believes the story I'm about to share with you was the catalyst for all of the experiences she has had since the following event happened. She claims it opened her mind just enough to make her aware of things we cannot always explain.

She starts her story with eyes begging to be believed. "It was mid-April 1998 and my son and I were staying with my mother at her home in Sunrise off of University Drive, while my husband was going through basic training," she started.

None of them had ever had an unusual encounter in the house up to this point. "We had lived in the home for six years prior to the encounter I am about to describe," she went on. "I still go to sleep with the TV going as I have done since I was a kid, and usually my mom would come check on me and turn it off. She still does to this day even though I'm in my thirties and am rarely home. My mother is blind and requires my care and, therefore, I try to always be sure we were always safely locked in our home and secure every night."

"I was sleeping good this particular night," she said. "I remember waking up to the feeling of someone sitting at the foot of my bed and I could feel the pressure on my lower legs and feet. When I looked up I thought it was just my mom sitting there looking at me to make sure I was OK as all mothers seem to do when their baby is nearby. It didn't really faze me and I went on back to sleep. When I woke up in the morning, my TV was still on. I thought that was kind of odd because she didn't turn it off like she usually does. I walked back to her room and found my mom blow-drying her hair. I asked her if I could talk to her a minute, so she stopped working on her shoulder-length, golden, slightly graying hair and asked me if something was wrong. I then looked at her and asked why had she come into my room and sat at the foot of my bed during the night. She was silent with a confused expression on her lovely slightly aged face."

She then asked her why she left her TV on. "She looked like a deer caught in the headlights, and asked me what on earth was I talking about. So I asked again, and she said that she hadn't come in my room all night."

They went back and forth for a few minutes until her twelve-year-old son woke up and asked what they were talking about. "So I asked him if he had come into my room and he also said no," she continued. "I had this chill come over me and I told them both to quit messing with me and tell me the truth. They both denied coming in. I knew that it wasn't my son since he was only around seventy-five pounds and the weight on the bed felt closer to my mother's two-hundred-pound figure."

Her mother started to get a little worried seeing as how she was clearly freaked out. "She asked me what all I remembered and if I could tell her exactly what I saw. I started telling them both what I could recall. Then it hit me. I had opened my eyes and saw someone sitting at the foot of my bed looking at me, but it didn't scare me at the time. I also recalled that I could see my TV on through the person sitting on my bed. At the time, I was so tired that I did not register the oddity. The best way I could describe it was that it looked at me in a way that was like someone tending to an ill child or a patient. It was in no way menacing. I really couldn't make out many facial features since I only saw it for a couple of seconds and I was woke up from a sound sleep. This is why I simply think my tired mind assumed it was my mother."

Lindsey exhaled a deep breath that she seemed to have been holding in for a minute after her tale. She seemed almost catatonic as she waited to see how her story was accepted. I accepted her story. Then she continued, "This particular night with a strange and unexplained nightly visitor may have been forgotten with time. In fact, my brain even may have remembered it all as a dream in time if my mother hadn't made a crucial mistake when trying to put my mind at ease. She told me that I was likely dreaming the whole encounter. She went on to say because my mind was having a hard time trying to recall the dream that was the fear I was feeling.

"Just when I was starting to feel better, my mother said something that turned my knees to Jell-o! She said that if she been really her checking on me, she would have stroked my hair and held my hand for awhile before leaving the room, just like I did for her two nights earlier. For the first time I was happy my sweet mother could not see me and grateful my son was old enough to steady me before shock nearly had me falling to the floor. I had never been in her room two nights earlier and my son was at his dad's!"

When through with sharing her story, Lindsey stood to her full five-foot, three-inch frame and fidgeted with the gold chain around her neck. She woke the following morning with a god-awful feeling words could not describe. Later, she found out that the man and his wife who built the home they were living in had been arrested. The man was serving a twenty-five-year sentence for molesting three foster girls. The wife had been stabbed and killed while serving her sentence. The young victims claimed they would come into their rooms at night as they slept and start out sitting on the bottom of their beds before reaching out to stroke their hair. To this day Lindsey claims she can never be alone. Despite the idea that the entity seemed harmless enough, she felt violated in an awkward kind of way that she just can't get over. A few months later, Lindsey's son claimed to have been woken by the nightly visitor—that was the breaking point. The family sold the house for a huge loss and moved on, leaving the visitor in the night behind.

"Both of my parents looked panicked as I told them what I remembered, and even went and checked all the doors and such to be sure no one had gotten in the house," she concluded. "But if that would've been the case, why on earth would someone come sit on my bed and look at me and do nothing else? I still don't know whose ghost it was, but I like to think that it was one of my close relatives who had passed on just coming in to check on me now that my husband was gone. Thinking of it that way makes it a little less creepy for me."

LIGHTS OVER THE FLORIDA TURNPIKE

Many stories circulated about strange sights and happenings along the Florida Turnpike. In the many years John C. patrolled this area, he'd never seen anything strange except for a twenty-one-second interval one night while on patrol.

This night, something drew his attention skyward. Whether it was lights or he just happened to look up, he just didn't know.

The object he saw was one thousand feet to fifteen hundred feet high and looked to be fifteen to twenty feet across. The object was very lit up and sparkled like old-time Christmas lights at the rear of this unidentified flying object, aka UFO. The object appeared to be hovering before suddenly bolting across the sky.

Within fifteen seconds, it was gone. The dazzling lights left him dumbfounded. He was so anxious to see someone, to ask them if he had seen what he saw or what he thought he had seen. A minute later, a Chevy van approached. He turned on his lights and sirens and pulled the minivan over.

When he approached the vehicle, he saw a woman and two children inside. The woman had a puzzled look on her face, "Did I do something wrong, officer?" she asked.

He told her that she had not broken any laws, but he was just wondering if she witnessed any strange lights in the sky. A child in the back seat of about nine years old spoke up before she could answer, "Mom, I told you there was a UFO!"

The woman went on to say that a few minutes before being pulled over her two sons insisted they'd seen a UFO in the sky. She did not see anything herself. After a few moments of conversation, he let the mother go on her way.

Even though he was convinced that he was wide awake and alert, the kids' testimony of what they seen helped confirm his belief. He decided not to mention the incident to anyone. Later, a fellow turnpike patrolman told of seeing the same sight or object. Over the years, strangely in October—the same month he witnessed the lights—many claims of lights in the sky were given as excuses from drivers he'd pulled over. The witnesses were often the drivers that seemed to swerve from one lane to another as they continued to search the sky.

All witnesses gave almost identical descriptions. To this day, John remembered what the object looked like. He didn't know what it was, but he knew that he had never seen anything like it before or since.

The Haunted Arcade

Often arcades are full of children and adults alike. The idea of enjoying a healthy rush, the challenge most video games offer, seldom brings the player nightmares. The Gameworks Arcade located in the Sawgrass Mills Mall area is the ideal arcade for anyone looking for some family fun. There you will laugh and enjoy the games, leaving with smiles on your faces—unless you have the misfortune of running into the arcade's ghost!

In March of 2010, Greg and Natasha Lewis where having a great time at Gameworks with their eight-year-old twin boys. They had been there about two hours when suddenly they had a confrontation that gave the boys nightmares for months.

The haunted Gameworks Arcade is located in Sawgrass Mills Mall, which is owned by Simon Malls. *Courtesy of W.C. Madden.*

The directory to the Sawgrass Mills Mall tells one where the Gameworks Arcade is located. *Courtesy of W.C. Madden.*

Greg was enjoying a game while his wife and sons watched. Suddenly, in the screen of the game the family had just been looking at with enthusiasm appeared the image of a boy! The Lewis family froze and looked in disbelief. The boy was the color of mocha and about ten years old. What made the image ghastly was the long open wound on the side of his face! The wound ran from the left side of his chin to the hairline of his head. There was blood and fat tissue protruding in the horrific image. His eyes appeared vacant as he looked directly at the Lewis family. Greg turned around, looking behind them and all around the arcade.

Despite the arcade being packed, there was no one that fit the image of the boy. Looking back at the video game, the boy still appeared as if he was just behind the glass. The game seemed to go on behind his image. Greg and Natasha exchanged glances. Greg grabbed the arm of a young man passing by and asked him what he saw in the video game. The young man looked puzzled and said he had seen the game.

The boy had vanished—there was no sign of him anywhere! The family had enough video games for the time being and left as fast as they could. About a week later, Mr. Lewis returned by himself. He asked a man that was working there if he'd ever heard of anyone else having a similar experience. The man replied that he had not and made it obvious that he thought Greg was not playing with a full deck. As Greg was leaving, a young woman who had overheard the conversation approached him. She worked part time at Gameworks and told him that a while back some teenagers had complained to her about a boy that had eerily appeared in their video game. She thought they were just pulling her leg and thought no more of it until Greg appeared with his encounter!

So the next time you are enjoying a video game at the Gameworks arcade, keep your eyes peeled for the boy who haunts the machines. You may get a thrill that will haunt your dreams for the months that follow! Regardless, the pizza and fun you will find at the Gameworks arcade in the Sawgrass Mills Mall is well worth the risk, if you dare!

CHAPTER 6

HOLLYWOOD HAUNTS

CELEBRITY GHOST AT THE CASINO

Although many ghost sightings take place at old places, a place doesn't have to be old to be haunted. Take the Seminole Hard Rock Casino in Hollywood for instance.

Opened on May 11, 2004, this South Florida entertainment complex stands twelve-stories high and covers eighty-six acres of Seminole tribe land. The casino is part of the Hard Rock franchise that began as the Hard Rock Cafe in London, England. This hotel gives the illusion of heaven on earth. In a word, the Seminole Hard Rock Hotel and Casino is splendid!

The casino came to international attention on February 8, 2007, when a celebrity who was staying at the casino's hotel died in her room. Anna Nicole Smith was the *Playboy* Playmate of the Year 1993. She had the Marylyn Monroe appeal; the stunning buxom blond with sexy, full lips was bound to make headlines. She could not have existed unnoticed.

She was a B-movie actress, a model, reality-TV star, widowed heiress, diet-pill spokesperson and tabloid darling. Smith died in room 607 on the sixth floor of this hotel. On February 8, 2007, at 1:38 p.m., Anna's bodyguard, Maurice "Big Moe" Brighthaupt, called the hotel's front desk and told the clerk that he'd found Anna Nicole unconscious and unresponsive. The clerk called 911. Anna was transported by ambulance to Memorial Regional Hospital where she was pronounced

The Seminole Hard Rock Casino now has a celebrity ghost. *Courtesy of W.C. Madden.*

dead on arrival. The cause of death was ruled to be "combined drug intoxication" from taking a number of different pills, including a sleep aid, human growth hormone and a variety of antidepressants and anti-anxiety medication. A large number of prescription medications were discovered in her room.

Smith's death came only months after the birth of her daughter, Hannibel (Hannah) Rose Hogan (renamed Dannielynn Hope Marshall Stern within a month of her birth), and the nearly simultaneous death of her adult son, Daniel Smith. Daniel had died a mere three days after his sister (twenty years his junior) had been born. Daniel died in a similar manner as his mother; an autopsy revealed his death to have been caused by a fatal combination of drugs, including methadone. Depression over the death of her son may have played a factor in the events leading to Anna's own death.

After the death of Anna Nicole, a very dramatic and public legal struggle ensued over the actual biological father of Anna's daughter Dannielynn. Four men claimed paternity of the child and two other men, including Smith's long-deceased oil tycoon husband J. Howard Marshall, were theorized to also be potential fathers of the little girl. Ultimately, DNA testing revealed the child to be the daughter of Larry Birkhead, an ex-boyfriend of Anna Nicole's.

On March 12, 2009, Anna Nicole's lawyer and boyfriend Howard K. Stern was arrested along with Dr. Sandeep Kapoor on felony charges of conspiring to furnish controlled substances, unlawfully prescribing a controlled substance and obtaining fraudulent prescriptions. Another doctor, Khristine Eroshevich, has been named as a conspirator as well. California attorney general Jerry Brown has alleged that Stern worked with the doctors to provide Anna Nicole with illegally prescribed drugs.

Since Anna Nicole's death, the room in which she died has been gutted and remodeled. The room numbers for the entire sixth floor were also changed. The casino has gone to these lengths in the hopes that it will prevent tourists who wish to see or stay in the room in which Smith died. Workers of the hotel claim that all the wallpaper, furniture and artwork were burned in Anna Nicole's room because of the Seminoles' traditions of dealing with the dead.

There was an alleged ghost sighting at the hotel in 2008, *In Touch Weekly* magazine reported that a guest of the hotel claimed to have seen the spirit of Anna Nicole Smith wandering the hotel lobby during a New Year's celebration. There have been no other public claims of haunting at the casino. However, this isn't the only story tying Anna Nicole to the supernatural.

A few years prior to her death, Anna Nicole Smith granted an interview to British publication *FHM Magazine* for their July 2004 issue. In her interview she made the outrageous claim that she'd repeatedly had sex with a ghost. She told the magazine:

> *Well…a ghost would crawl up my leg and have sex with me at an apartment a long time ago in Texas. I used to think it was my boyfriend, then one day I woke up and found it wasn't. It was, like, a spirit. And it WOO!…went up! I was freaked out about it, but then I was, like, Well, you know what? He's never hurt me—and he just gave me some amazing sex, so I have no problem. It wasn't a dream, because it was happening every night!*

On another occurrence, a man staying on the sixth floor claimed that he had a late-night knock at the door. The man was a guest of the hotel and was in his early forties. At about midnight, he'd returned to his room to grab something. A moment after he entered the room, there was a light knock on the door. Opening the door, before his eyes was every man's dream come true! Standing tall and looking him directly in the eyes, was a beautiful and very naked woman. He was at a loss for words and found himself just staring back. The woman was the same height as him, five-foot-eleven. She had almost glowing blonde hair and the sexiest lips he'd ever seen. He cannot remember much else about her facial appearance because he was drawn to looking at her two perfect breasts. In fact, he remembers thinking she appeared to look cold, although the temperature was comfortable. Then—just like that—she evaporated before him into a mist that seemed to just dissolve!

After recovering himself, he found the nearest staff worker and told him what he had seen. The staff worker, Luis, told the man his was not

The Seminole Paradise is part of the Seminole Hard Rock Casino. *Courtesy of W.C. Madden.*

the first tale of ghost sightings on that floor he has heard. Luis claims the man checked out early that morning.

Not a week earlier, two of the housekeeping girls shared a frightening encounter with Luis that took place on the sixth floor. Apparently, the ladies had been making up a room when they heard a disembodied voice. The voice said, "Nice" and then in a very feminine sound, softly giggled. The girls left the room quickly.

Another housekeeping worker claims that the snack-size bag of Doritos chips she had with her when she was cleaning a room levitated. The bag lifted about a foot off the nightstand and stayed in the air for at least thirty seconds! Ironically, Doritos are said to have been one of Anna Nicole's favorite foods. The woman who witnessed the levitation of the chips can no longer stomach Doritos herself.

Another staff member claims to have been told by a very discreet guest that he awoke to the sound of two girls playing in his very room. Problem is he was alone in the room!

John, a maintenance worker, saw a beautiful blonde smile at him from the pool. She was dressed different from others that were around the pool, wearing a white silk bathrobe. As if she knew he was staring at her, she disrobed, revealing what he calls a vision of female perfection! He nearly fell in the pool but then he found himself on his knees. The nude woman dissolved and he realized no one else seemed to notice. He will never forget that moment!

Visitors to the casino will find plenty of things to do. Outside the casino, there is a 4.5-acre swimming pool created in the form of a lagoon. The pool has a beach-club pool bar in the middle. There have been claims of seeing a black mass floating above the water. In addition, a woman wearing a one-piece bath bathing suit with dark, shoulder-length hair has been described to Luis from other workers who have claimed to catch a glimpse of her by the cabanas.

Outside visitors will also find the Seminole Okalee Indian Village & Museum, which also presents the history, art and culture of the Seminoles. The village features a live animal show that includes local animals such as bears, panthers and snakes. The show is the only one in the world to feature deep-water alligator wrestling demonstrations. During one of these demonstrations, two sisters are certain they saw a tall Seminole man in original clothing from at least one hundred years ago, who then promptly disappeared. He had a stern and angry look on his face as he was eyeing the crowd. His angry expression is what got the girls' attention in the first place. Then suddenly he seemed to flicker and become transparent; and then he was gone!

Other reports have been bed covers being tugged at and mysterious drafts and sounds—dresser drawers that seem to open on its own and things that appear to have moved from its original location. Regardless of who may haunt the Seminole Hard Rock Hotel and Casino, it is easy to see why. This is a place one cannot imagine a soul is trapped. The ghost would appear to be enjoying the splendid accommodations. The Seminole hotel and casino may really be heaven on earth for some in the afterlife.

THE FATHERLY GHOST AT THE AIRPORT

For people who like to people watch, an airport is often a fun place to go. People from all over the world pass through the corridors of Fort Lauderdale-Hollywood International Airport wearing the fashions of their homelands. The airport processes more than twenty-two million people a year and more than three million from foreign lands.

The airport can trace its roots back to 1929, when Merle Fogg Airport was built on the site of an abandoned nine-hole golf course. When World War II began, the United States Navy took it over and commissioned it as Naval Air Station Fort Lauderdale. It was used for training. On October 1, 1946, the navy turned the base over to civilian authorities, who renamed it Broward County International Airport. After Hollywood grew to a large city, the airport was renamed again.

Stephanie Anderstand is one of those people who like to go and watch people. Once a week since she was a child, she would go to the airport with her dad, Steve, and just sit and watch the people. They would create stories about where they were from and what their lives might be like. This was a special time for the two of them, and Stephanie looked forward to it every month. The two would find a different spot to sit every time, and they'd laugh over some people and tell each other great adventure stories about others.

When Stephanie was nineteen, her father passed away. She still kept the tradition alive and continued to go to Fort Lauderdale-Hollywood International Airport to people watch on a monthly basis. She sat and watched the people passing by and felt strangely close to her dad. This had a soothing affect on her.

On Stephanie's thirtieth birthday, she was feeling very sad and deeply missed her father. Although she had already been to the airport the week before, she decided to go again. She entered the airport wearing her favorite pair of size seven blue jeans on her tall, five-foot, eleven-inch frame and her dad's denim jacket with an eagle patch on the arm. She was an ordinary girl with brown hair pulled back in a ponytail and brown eyes. No one ever seemed to notice her as she found a comfortable spot to sit.

On this particular day, about five minutes after she sat down, Stephanie noticed a strong odor. The distinct smell of Aqua Velva cologne filled her nostrils. Her senses automatically triggered memories of her father; this was the cologne he always wore. Also, the smell of Camel cigarettes seemed to mix with the smell of the cologne. This raised the hairs on the back of her neck. Stephanie remembered as a child hugging her father and smelling those two things. For some reason unknown to her, she felt safe and had a feeling of home overcome her.

A few minutes passed as she sat there taking in the calming smell and reflecting on her youth when a tickle came across her cheek and a cool breeze blew past her. The tickle reminded her so much of the way her father's moustache felt against her cheek when he'd give her a kiss.

Stephanie was feeling so relaxed when a young gift shop attendant approached her. She was short and pudgy with a sweet face and seemed nervous. She asked Stephanie if she realized there was a man sitting right beside her just a moment ago. Stephanie told her she had been sitting alone for the last ten minutes and asked why she had asked such a strange question. The young girl went on to explain that she worked in the gift shop nearby. She said a few months ago she started noticing this man sitting by himself a lot and people watching. He always sat in a different spot and seemed harmless but had caught her attention. She said there was something different about the man, but could not put her finger on it. Then she went on to say that five minutes earlier, she had seen him sit unusually close to Stephanie. What was odd to her was that Stephanie did not even seem to acknowledge him as he sat staring directly at her side profile. Then the man reached an arm around Stephanie's back and gave her a kiss on the cheek before disappearing into thin air.

The girl pointed over to the gift shop at the postcards she'd dropped when she seen this happen. Stephanie made eye contact with the girl and asked what the man looked like. She said he was tall and broad in frame with brown hair and eyes. She looked at Stephanie's jacket with the eagle patch on the arm and said he had on the exact same jacket and khaki pants. Stephanie's eyes began to water and said, "You have just described my deceased father."

Stephanie still continues to go to the airport once a month almost five years later. Over time, she has felt her father's moustache tickle her cheek half a dozen times. She is happy to think her father still meets her at a place they were so happy together for her special time. The young gift shop worker told Stephanie months after the incident that she seen him one day sitting beside a little girl who later turned out to be lost. Security claims a nice man told her to just sit with him and wait until she was found. No doubt Stephanie's father was a loving and caring man who felt children were a precious gift and still enjoys looking out for them, even in the afterlife.

CHAPTER 7

MIRAMAR HAUNTS

THE HAUNTED SNAKE WARRIOR'S ISLAND

In early 2010, the movie *Shutter Island* was released, starring Leonardo DiCaprio. The scary movie was about an island in Boston Harbor. Broward County has a scary island as well called Snake Warrior's Island.

The park in Miramar is part of the Great Florida Birding Trail; it's an excellent place for bird-watching and to maybe spot a ghost or two.

At one time the park was an island in the Everglades. Cuban ranchers were first on the island in the 1700s. They put in a boat landing; then they raised hogs and cattle and shipped them back to Cuba.

A sea captain tried to establish a trading post there in the early 1800s to do business with the Indians. But that wasn't successful. "The Indians called the place an evil island and they wouldn't come there," said Robert W. Fritchey in the *Miami Herald*. The captain closed up shop since the Indians wouldn't come there.

However, the Seminoles decided to take over the island in 1828 and named it after Snake Warrior Chitto Tustenuggee. Snake Warrior Island became the seasonal home of the popular and gregarious leader Old Tiger Tail, the bitter veteran Old Alec and the dashing Young Tiger Tail.

In the 1850s, Pete Tiger poignantly discussed the situation with a *Reader's Digest* columnist:

> *In the old times we could paddle our canoes for many days and hunt the deer and the alligator. Now the white man has drained the Glades with his canals to make fields for his tomatoes and sugarcane. Our canoes cannot run on the sand and it is forbidden to cross the white man's fences. And the deer and the alligator each day go farther away.*

Drainage operations finally drove the Seminoles out in the 1890s. White settlers took over and saw mysterious lights on the north side of the island. Some folks though they were haints (the southern word for ghosts).

In the 1920s, a group of African Americans were gathering rocks from the island for home construction in North Dade and were frightened off by a strange apparition. "They said they saw an old slave ship sail up to the old boat landing, and it was full of haints trying to catch them," Fritchey said.

Then there was an old hermit who lived there. Some people swore they head moaning and groaning coming from the island.

Ghostly rumors about the island kept farmers from planting too close to it. A surveying crew felt they were being watched by someone on the island, so they went to it to find the person. "They never found anybody," said Garth Fripps in the *Miami Herald*. "Not even any footprints."

The now landlocked island is just north of Pro Player Stadium in Broward County. People go there looking for birds, not ghosts.

CHAPTER 8

TAMARAC HAUNTS

HAUNTED TOWNHOUSE

Ever since the Lopez family moved into their three-bedroom townhouse in Tamarac, a lot of spirit and ghostly sightings have occurred. People who are sensitive and have visited their house have told many of what they have seen. They have seen dark shadows, a small child, an elderly woman and paranormal activities such as pots and pans banging in the kitchen, TVs turning off or changing channels and fans turning on without prompting. These are just a few examples of the many odd events that have plagued the family.

The latest events have been very weird. One night, the recently divorced and eldest daughter woke up to a sound in front of the bed she slept in. There was a dark figure standing at the foot of her bed. Her four-year-old son, who slept in the next bed, was sitting in the bed and pointing at the figure and telling her, "Look, Mom. What's that?"

After he repeated this about three times, his mother found her voice and told him to just go to sleep and that he was dreaming, but she also saw it. As soon as he went back to sleep, she looked back and the figure was gone.

About a month later, her son woke her up saying, "Look, Mom! Look at that!"

He kept pointing to the front of her bed and following it with his finger pointing until the shadow left their room. Then he asked her if they could follow it to see where it was going. She just told him to please go to sleep, that he was dreaming again, but she admits she was too scared to get up and find out more.

A few weeks later, her son woke her up and said, "Mom! Mom! Wake up! Look!"

He was standing in the bed and had the blanket in front of him like he was trying to block the black figure in front of him. As soon as she woke up and saw the figure, it disappeared into the darkness.

About three days later, she was very restless and kept dreaming about spirits in the house. They kept opening the front doors of the house and she kept running in the halls and telling them to leave. One of the spirits kicked a ball in the hall and for an unknown reason she was very scared about that.

The next day her mom asked her why she was arguing all night! She told her she was telling the spirits to leave the house in her dream, while her seventeen-year-old brother told her he had woken up at 3 in the morning and had gone into the hallway and kicked one of her son's shoes. When he bent down to pick it up, he felt a hard, cold draft of air like someone had just passed, running in front of him. Then the sound of a ball bouncing passed by where he stood. So real was this that he could feel the floor vibrate.

The Lopez family has never solved the mysteries of their haunted townhouse. Also, they don't know why, but all these things always seem to happen at 3 in the morning. The family has woken up to all the faucets in the house turned on full blast at that time. Also, toilets will flush in both bathrooms when no one is in them. Strange as the events are, the family loves the community, and they have no intention of leaving—ghost or no ghost. The townhouse is located on San Carlos Circle.

About the Authors

Dorothy (Salvo) Davis is the author of two previous books, *Ghost Stories of White County* and *Haunted Lafayette*. She graduated from Deerfield Beach High School in Deerfield, Florida. She moved to Wolcott, Indiana, in 2003 and then to Monticello, Indiana, in 2006. She is a wife and mother. Her hobbies include soccer, Girl Scouts and gardening. She is a history buff and enjoys researching various time periods. Raised in an Italian American family, her favorite historical subject is the Roman Empire.

W.C. Madden is an accomplished author with thirty books and more than one hundred magazine articles to his credit. He has a journalism degree from Our Lady of the Lake University, San Antonio, Texas. He's a member of the White

County Historical Society, Monticello Rotary and Monticello Kiwanis. He first began writing for publication in the United States Air Force and won the prestigious Thomas Jefferson Award for his writing in the military. He was also an award-winning journalist with the *Noblesville Ledger* in Noblesville, Indiana.

www.ingramcontent.com/pod-product-compliance
Lightning Source LLC
Chambersburg PA
CBHW060622310726
48982CB00003B/637

9781540234841